Trapped in l'Acadie

a Kesk8a story

www.crowecreations.ca

Trapped in l'Acadie
© 2020 Sherrill Wark

First Crowe Creations Print Publication December 2020.

This is a work of fiction set against a backdrop of history. Except for actual historical persons (e.g., Benjamin Church, Queen Anne, King Louis XIV, etc.), almost all characters are fictional so any resemblance to persons living or dead is a coincidence. And even the opinions about actual historical persons (e.g., those about Benjamin Church) are those of fictional characters, not this author's. This author's actual ancestors, Claude Guidry and Marguerite Petitpas, and their son, J-B, were real. Kesk8a was real, too.

Front cover photo © iStock, photo ID:0000614667
Cover Design © 2020 Crowe Creations
Interior design by Crowe Creations
Text set in Garamond; headings in Clarity Gothic SF

Crowe Creations
ISBN: 978-1-927058-73-2

Dedicated to the Black Lives Matter Movement

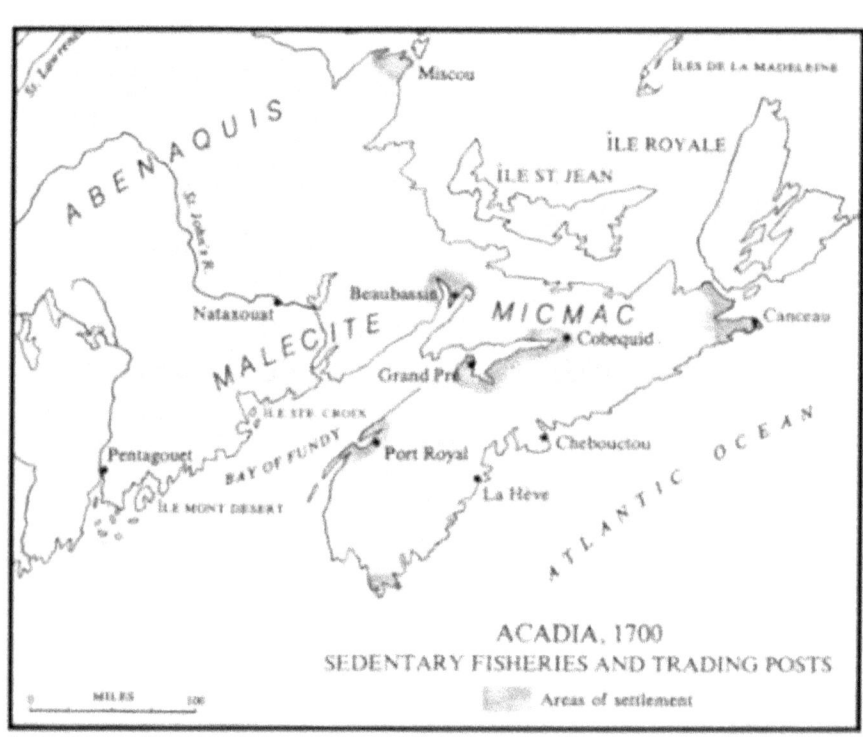

ACADIA, 1700
SEDENTARY FISHERIES AND TRADING POSTS

Areas of settlement

"But what we hope
does not always come to be."—Keskoua

Foreword

Believing it would be the most authentic way of setting up the world of Acadia, for the first two books in the Kesk8a series I chose my characters' names by doing an Internet search for 17th-century-France surnames and given names, then added a soupçon of names from other countries (Portugal, Spain, The Netherlands, England, Scandinavia, et cetera) whose sailors, or their offspring, might have ended up on Acadia's shores because of whatever adventures—or, more likely, misadventures—might have befallen them. Those who have read these first two books will know that most of these characters were killed off by Karma and history anyway, so all was well for this author.

By book 3, however, the population of Acadia has both grown and shrunk name-wise. (From Jim Bradshaw's *Les Doucet du Monde*: "There were between 4,000 and 5,000 Acadians in 1730, more than double the population of 1710." http://doucetfamily.org/heritage/Heritage.htm) My dilemma now was to invent characters' names drawn from authentic Acadian surnames and given names without coming up with any real persons' names.

Impossible.

Now how can I handle this? In any book there has to be conflict. Characters have to do bad things that are good-meaning and some that aren't. In historical novels about Acadia and its conflict with New

England, people kill people. In real life people cheat others, people lie, people rape, people steal, people run around on their spouses. People get diseases. (Syphilis was documented in Europe as early as 1495.) How would I set all this up without offending any of my millions of *cousines*? Without having readers contact me with "I'll have you know that my 6th great grandfather was NOT in Grand Pré at that time and neither was any member of his family. Your research sucks."

I'm sorry, I am writing *fiction* and it is historical fiction, so the backdrop of my fictional stories has to be as accurate as I can get it without making my readers fall asleep. I take some liberties, for example with who currently occupies the fort at Port Royal because it changed hands practically every weekend (France, England, The Netherlands...), but in general it's accurate. As accurate as it can be. Never forget that old saying: "History is written by the victor."

My goal in writing this series is to show things from the other side, how people survived the atrocities heaped upon all of them, on the Mi'qmaw and Newcomers alike, and in later books, their mixed offspring, and how they remained *une famille* in spite of it all.

Every Acadian family has a Jean-Baptiste in it somewhere. The second son of my first ancestor from France (arrived Port Royal ca. 1670) was Jean-Baptiste Guidry. I need him for book 4, *The Hanging.* He was real, as were his parents, Claude Guédry and Marguerite Petitpas. Kesk8a was real and had a child with Claude, but I believe she died in childbirth ca. 1680. I have kept her alive because she would have wanted it that way. She's the one telling the stories. She's the one who, when I first learned of her, reached out and grabbed my heart and squeezed as she laughingly gave me the first line in the first book: "When I told my friend Feather that I wanted to lay with the Father, she was horrified and told me I had to go to Confession right away or I'd go to Hell for sure. 'And I told you,' she added. 'Don't call me Feather no more. Call me Hélène.'"

In this book and in the following three, I will try my best to use only the surnames from my own tree when I am writing about made-up Acadians. I've done my family research with the help of Denis Cyr (https://www.acadian.org/), Ancestry.com, MyHeritage and Geni, so as of ca. 1730s and earlier for this book, *c'est ma famille*: Baduel, Bagard, Bajolet, Baudinet, Bayol, Blain, Boucher, Branger, Brasseau, Bugaret, Comeau, Demers, Desmarais, Dugas, d'Entremont, Forest, Gaudet, Gingras, Granger, Guédry/Guidry, Guibeau, Hebert, La Bine, Lafranchise, Landry, Mace, Martineau, Melançon/Melanson, Petitpas, Picotte, Rocheron, St-Martin and Thibodeau. First names in my tree are: Adelaide, Anne, Antoine, Augustin, Barbe, Bernard, Catherine, Cecile, Celeste, Charles, Claude, Daniel, Elizabeth, Firmin, François, Françoise, Gabrielle, Isaac, Isabelle, Jacques, Jean, Jean-Baptiste, Jeanne, Joseph, Louis, Marguerite, Marie Anne, Marie-Josephe, Martin, Michel, Oliner, Paul, Pierre, Raymond and Therese.

If I ended up writing about some murdering [literal] bastard [literal] named Jean d'Eau who gave his wife and daughter syphilis—and maybe his son and his grandmother, too—and this was your ancestor and he actually did do this, I'm sorry. It was not my intention to out him. It is, as it says on the Copyright page, a coincidence.

SW
2020

Near Port Royal, Acadia, summer, 1704

One

Benny was back in our midst. This time not as a false slave hunter, but as himself: Colonel Benjamin Church, New England Ranger. And he was attacking us. For several moons, even over our own cooking fires, we had smelled the smoke that came all the way across the Big Bay from the land of the Maliseet. But this time, the stench was coming from the northeast.

I went to talk to our Chief to see if he'd heard anything from the soldiers at the fort.

"You're the one who usually gives all that information to them." Singing Bear had no meanness in his voice. It held a question. "Still no pigeon message from your friend in Boston?"

I shook my head. "Not for three days now. I'm worried."

"If it will make you feel better, no one at the fort has had any pigeons come in either. From anywhere." He looked at me from under one eyebrow as he bent to re-tie the strap around his right ankle. I hadn't noticed it had become undone.

"Will they ever stop?" I asked.

"Who? The pigeons?"

I didn't laugh. "The New Englanders, the English. Will they ever stop?"

"Not while an Acadian house or church or cow or chicken or stalk of wheat remains standing."

"Why do they hate them so much?" I watched him re-tie the strap around his other ankle. Bear was hiding something from me.

"You know as well as I the answer to that question." He rose to his full height which was slightly more than mine.

I asked him straight out. "You're going somewhere. You're going to talk to Gabbie at the fort, aren't you?"

"Don't you have things to do? Like go collect plants or something?"

"All I need is some kaksk´us, cedar. I'll collect that later. Maybe even tomorrow. Right now? I'm coming with you. The people are getting sick from all the smoke. I need to know what he's going to do about it."

As we approached the fort—for the last few years now, wide open and devoid of surrounding trees, bushes, buildings and wikuoms—what sounded like men's voices raised in anger reached us.

"Some kind of fight going on," I said, more or less to myself. "Again."

Several cracks told me that weapons were being fired.

"Another raid. Come this way." Singing Bear grabbed my arm to pull me back into those trees that still surrounded the area of the fort. "We'll have to approach from around behind on this side. I don't want to get my head shot off."

"And I don't want to get splattered with your brains. I just finished making this." I patted my deerskin jacket. It wasn't cold enough yet to be wearing it, even at night, but I was proud of the quillwork on it.

We both laughed but not because anything was funny.

As we lowered ourselves onto our stomachs behind a fallen tree, Bear asked the same question everybody else had been asking me for six moons: "Has your wonderful, charming, protective, responsible, loveable, perfect husband, Falcon, returned to his senses yet?"

"You know the answer to that as well as I do, Bear." I whispered this because we were close enough to the fighting to be overheard. The men at the fort were so nervous these days, they'd shoot into the trees if a chipmunk passed wind. I didn't want my head shot off either.

"Of course, I know. I'm just trying to get you to talk about it."

"Ah. So now you are giving counsel and guidance to *me*." What my husband had done was one path I did not want to travel along with anybody, especially with Singing Bear.

"Well, Keskoua?"

"Listen!"

Men's voices rising in cheers bounced off the snawe'g, the sugar trees, in the bush behind us. I didn't know whether to be relieved or frightened. "Which side is cheering? Can you recognize any words? English? French?"

One shot rang out. A cry of pain in the distance. Laughter, then the silence of victory.

"Keskoua?"

"App? What?" Would this man never give up?

"I am Chief. I give counsel and guidance to everyone."

"I can take care of this myself."

"With him away you have no one else to talk to. You know. About serious personal issues."

"That's not true."

Lithe as a squirrel, Bear was on his feet extending his hands to help me up.

I didn't need his help. Not with getting onto my own feet or with getting the anger out of me about Falcon.

"I won't give up, Keskoua. I won't." Like a chickadee plucking a seed, he removed a bit of cedar off the front of my leather jacket. "With him away with her, you have no one to comfort you."

I started away toward the path that led to the fort, but he grabbed my arm to stop me.

"We have to talk about this, about Falcon."

"No we don't."

"We have to talk about us."

"There is no us."

"You know there is. You can't deny it."

Well… that much was true.

Two

There were three hundred soldiers at the fort. Not that I counted them. History did. Soldiers? They were children. Innocent. The Dutch New Englanders called them *bumpkins*. It was a word used for just about anybody who wasn't Dutch so didn't know Dutch ways. It was also what the English New Englanders called the Dutch New Englanders because they didn't know the English New Englanders' ways. I will never understand why people can make fun of each other just for being different from themselves, when they actually aren't different at all, only by their language and a few customs.

The soldiers at the fort had repulsed a raid once again but not without a lot of injuries this time. I always carried my munti with me—my bag of healing herbs and ointments—so rather than talk with Gabbie right away about the lack of pigeon messages from Boston and everywhere else, I helped Monsieur Coté, the surgeon, with the wounded. I was not surprised to see that Singing Bear had made a similar decision and was leading those men who could still walk to cots that people were setting up near the entrance to the surgeon's quarters. I counted thirty walking; seventeen unable to walk; eleven probably already dead by the slack of mouth, the open eyes, the gray shade to the skin. I hoped we could bury these before the next wave of raiders made it impossible to leave the fort to do so. Mourning ceremonies and funeral Masses would have to wait.

As I looked at the silent, unmoving, unbreathing bodies of these young men and wondered how their families were going to feel when they learned they'd never see their son, brother, husband, father again, a question went through my own head: Would I feel better if Falcon had died like these men had instead of leaving me for her? I would still be without him. Would the reason for it matter?

Like I said, it had started six moons ago and I might as well come right out with it and tell it the way it was. My beloved Falcon had started drinking alcohol again and had joined forces with the troubled Second Son. I'm not going to say that Second Son got Falcon going back to the bottle because I don't know. All I know for sure is that they took up with two sisters. Sad sisters who had been abused by drunken fathers and uncles and passers-through, and who were needing food so were trading "comfort" for it. As is our way, our people offered them food every day and my brother, Gi´gwesu, and his woman, Wasueg, had even built an extra wikuom for the two girls, but they didn't last very long there. As a healer, I knew many things about how people think, but the one that always puzzled me the most was how a woman who was damaged as a child by men could continue to offer her body to them. Did she believe her private region was the only thing of value she had? Was she trying to soothe the beast in them? What was it? Fear then? Or shame? Did she hope to overcome the shame as if by repeating the actions it would make everything na to´q, all right? Suddenly acceptable?

Second Son had already developed a following of young men—boys, really—fresh from their Spirit Quests and full of enthusiasm about protecting the community from any danger, especially from the Maudits anglaises. Yes, we all had begun to refer to the English from away and from the south of us with the same term as our French brothers did. Although our new priest, Père Abreo, never actually used that phrase in our presence, his unspoken support did nothing toward dousing Second Son's fire for fighting. The New Englanders were Protestants.

***

I'm not going to tell you this next part as a storyteller because for one thing I didn't see it myself, I only heard it from someone who heard it from someone else who heard it from someone else. The story about what people south of us were doing to their New England neighbors was so disturbing, I didn't want to remember it for even as long as a mayfly lives let alone keep it in my head to pass down to future generations. I'm only going to say it once to get it out. It had nothing to do with us in Acadia, but we in Acadia were included with the ones who took the brunt of the revenge. I already told you about people who make fun of anyone who doesn't believe the same things they do, or dress the same or talk the same. If you're doing something that isn't right, and you know in your heart it isn't right, you have one choice in front of you: do it or don't do it. If you want to make a lot of money trapping rabbits and selling their skins, you need a lot of rabbits. But if you take too many rabbits, there soon won't be any left. But if you want a lot of money bad enough, you'll do it anyway and take the guilty feelings with it. What would make it a lot easier, with no bad feelings, would be if somebody told you there was nothing wrong with it, that there was a whole book written that said there was nothing wrong with it. That it's na to´q, all right, to hate people who don't believe in the same things you do.

When the Newcomers first came to our village, they wanted to learn from us how to live in the bush and we were wanting to learn their ways, too. When the Fathers came, they told us we were wrong about everything and tried to make us change our ways—and many of us did. My friend, Hélène, once called Feather, was one of them. I was not. Some of the Fathers took on many of our ways and didn't push theirs on us as hard as others did. *Most* of them didn't. A few of the Fathers were so full of hate for Protestants, though, they encouraged our people to attack the New Englanders and do things to them I won't put into your heads except to say that both sides took scalps and thought nothing of it.

This caused no end of troubles as some of the New Englanders fought against every "Indian" they came across, even us around Port Royal who were minding our own business. Second Son was full of wind and made threats against the New Englanders, but he was also so full of alcohol, it was mostly only talk as he couldn't stand on his feet let alone lead a group of young men for days and days through unknown bush. Second Son made a lot of bad decisions, but I have to give him credit for not leading all our young men to a certain death in a strange land like our people south of us did.

The soldiers at the fort did as good a job as they could of keeping the Maudits anglaises from taking over. They would lose the fort for a while and then take it back again. I sometimes thought, if Port Royal were a woman, she would be a vain one having people fight over her all the time like that.

But it got so bad with the raids against the New Englanders—and it had been going on for many years—that the New Englanders asked their new Queen for help. They knew she would help them because she owned the land there and would want to keep owning it. (I still think somebody owning the land is a very strange way of seeing things, but that doesn't make me want to kill them.)

So the new Queen sent more and more ships and soldiers to attack the people. These ships and soldiers didn't attack only those who were attacking New England, they also attacked the settlements at Québec and Montréal and at Port Royal and Big Meadow again and again and again. Both sides were right. Both sides were wrong.

***

No matter which way we turned, there was fighting. Because of what a few crazy people—"Indians"—were doing in the name of "God" at the southern boundaries of Acadia, the New Englanders decided they might as well hate all of us, not just the French. The English couldn't tell us apart anymore because so many of us were mixed. Or maybe they did know, but didn't care.

This, of course, spurred on Second Son who didn't need much spurring on to start with. His bad reputation caused many to distrust him, except for our fresh young Spirit Questers, that is. And also, unfortunately, he had convinced my husband, Falcon, to join their forces. Falcon was "dynamic" (a new word for me), much loved and respected. People listened to him. Falcon was kind and forgiving of everyone. Second Son needed his help, Falcon offered it, then slipped into the bottomless lake of trouble.

Agada and Solange couldn't have been more than fifteen or sixteen winters old. Agada's hair flowed well past her shoulders and was so pale yellow it was almost white, and her eyes were such pale blue it was hard to read her mood from them; I couldn't see them. Solange's hair was the color of a wowkwis's shoulders, a red fox, and so short it would be impossible to pull it out. The bones under their skin made them look like each other, but nothing else looked like anybody else I'd ever seen in my life. My old friend Claude Guidry had green eyes, but they were nowhere near the color of Solange's green eyes. Hers flashed as brightly as her hair did. I could see why men would desire these girls: they were different, something new, something to examine, understand, pursue, conquer.

Falcon was over forty winters old and already thinking that his life was going to come to an end sooner than later. I understood his interest in being with the young men and helping train them in the ways of the bush and the ways of protecting our village; it was our way for the older people to help the young people learn. But to see him walk away into the arms of another woman—no matter her age—surprised and hurt me. We had a good relationship with each other, told each other everything. We still had fun on the cedars. What was he missing that I couldn't give him?

Three

By the time Monsieur Coté, Singing Bear and I had done our best with the injured soldiers, Sun was at the top of the sky. Many of the wounds were not serious, but there was always the worry of putrefaction. We had to perform only one amputation this time, a young man's leg. Fifteen were dead. The number would have risen to sixteen if we hadn't removed the boy's leg.

Singing Bear and I now had time to meet with Gabbie Grenier in his office. I must tell you that when I first met Gabbie, around the time Benny was here secretly hunting for information, I didn't know just how strong a man he would become. He had risen in the ranks at the fort and now held a high position. The raids on the fort were frequent, so the injuries to the men in his charge were frequent also. He bore all this without becoming sad and discouraged, and people respected him for this. Especially because, each time his King offered to bring him back to France, he declined. This always made me think of the former surgeon at the fort, a good friend, who was now living in Boston, under the false name of Edward Gooden, with his new wife. For several days now, I had received no pigeon messages from "Edward" about the secret activities going on there—mostly about what the Maudits anglaises might be planning to do to us here—and this made me worry for many reasons. He had never neglected to send a daily pigeon with information. Edward's first wife had remained in France when he came to Acadia. Had Gabbie and *his* wife annulled their marriage, too? Perhaps for the same reason? A child born too many months after the most-recent visit? Or without any visit home at all?

Gabbie knew enough of our language to get along but not enough to have a serious talk in, so we spoke French.

"I wish I had more news," he said, offering us chairs in front of the big *bureau* in his *bureau*. I sometimes laughed at how other languages said things. Not to be mean because I knew our language was strange to others, too, but today, something made me wonder if the desk in an office got its name first or if the office was named after the desk that was in it. Gabbie did not sit in his big chair but kept his back to us at the window behind his *bureau*, his desk. "No pigeons. No friendly ships with information. They are everywhere in the bush now, too, so it is not safe to send messengers even by land."

A soldier entered with a tray that he placed on Gabbie's desk before pouring a cup of tea for each of us. Bear asked for maple sugar in his and both of us asked for milk. Their tea always tasted better with milk. That's what I thought anyway.

"We've had no news, either," Bear said, taking a sip from his cup. "Hmm. Good." He closed one eye at me and whispered, "Surprisingly good."

I sipped my own and nodded agreement. "Thank you," I told the soldier, who bowed his head, clicked his heels together, saluted Gabbie's back, then departed.

"The only thing I can tell you is that we have captured a New England soldier and are now interrogating him."

The rapid knocking of what sounded like an apo'qatej, a woodpecker, looking for a suitable mate, sounded on Gabbie's door.

"Enter."

Into the room marched a young soldier I knew as Pierre Poitou,

Gabbie's nephew. The young soldier saluted. "We have obtained information from the prisoner, Sir."

Gabbie turned to face him. "You may speak. Singing Bear and Keskoua can be trusted. You know that."

"I'm sorry, Sir. I am to speak only to you, Sir."

"Very well." With an elegant sweep of his arm, Gabbie indicated the door. "Please accept my apologies." To me, he said, "You may take your tea with you, if you wish. You may even keep the cup."

I left my tea on Gabbie's desk and rose from my chair. I adjusted my munti on my shoulder as I stepped away.

Behind me, I heard him say to Bear, "Give us ten minutes." Then to the young soldier. "Oui?"

"Oui, Sir." Another salute and a click of heels and the young soldier was ahead of me to open the door to let me pass through. I heard the door shut behind me then open again before Bear was at my side.

Outside, we had just stepped through the gates out of the fort when a familiar voice caught my attention. "Ah, le voilà. There you are." It was Claude Guidry's wife, Marguerite Petitpas. "Have you seen him? Is he in there? Your brother told me he'd check with one of his friends. Did you see him?" She pushed past me to lean through the gates of the fort.

"Who? Claude?"

"No, no. J-B. Nobody knows where he is. Your brother's boys are looking, too. Your whole family is helping me. Except for you."

Bear had moved away leaving me to deal with Marguerite by myself. "Your son is probably in the bush searching with everybody else for messages on dead pigeons' legs."

"There is no everybody else anymore. The Maudits anglaises are watching the adults, so it's only the younger children looking for those poor dead creatures. To fool them, you know? Where have you been that you aren't aware of this?"

I didn't have an answer except that I had been too busy keeping people alive to worry about who was wandering around in the bush.

"Your brother Gig's boys are doing me a favor. At least he knows what's going on. Mon Dieu."

"When last did you see J-B? I haven't seen him for perhaps two days. Maybe three."

"I have a terrible feeling," said Marguerite, shaking her head. "I've been having cauchemars, nightmares. I…"

Bear's hand on my shoulder startled me. "Take her home. She's distraught."

"But what about Gabbie? Aren't we—?"

"I'll handle it. Take her home."

I didn't want to be sent away like a small child who wasn't to know the business of their parents, but I put my arm over Marguerite's shoulders and led her toward the path that would take us to hers and Claude's cabin. When I heard about people having nightmares, it was enough to give me nightmares, too. Especially now. Things were much more tense in this part of the land. I would go with her. I would make a special calming tea for her. Lemon balm. I knew Claude would be there. He'd been skinning a deer when I passed by early that morning.

"I'll go with you. To your cabin. I'll make tea." I patted my munti.

Her sigh came all the way from her toes. Then, skirts billowing like a sail in a storm, she strode away along the path.

As I followed quickly along behind her, I hoped in my heart that J-B would be safe and well. Not only for his mother's sake, but for mine, too. He was a good man. I liked him and so did everyone who met him.

The pigeon messages that had been getting through in late spring from northeast of us did not have good news in them. Many people were dying not only from the New England Rangers' guns and swords, but from the smoke of the fires they set. The messages were also telling us there was no food. We were not untouched here in Port Royal. Their smoke was drifting in so our people—both old and young—were having problems with breathing. Even some of our babies were being born with illnesses.

Marguerite led me toward the very familiar eating area inside her cabin with its huge, long table and many wooden chairs. Like a big fishing net settling on ocean waves, she lowered herself and her flowing skirts onto one of the chairs. I could see that her worrying about J-B was making her very tired.

"Vas-y, chère. Make me some of your special tea. Mon Dieu, I hope it does the trick."

The wood stove was always going, even in the summer, but between meals, like now, it had only embers in it. I knew about fires, of course, but not much about wood stoves. Especially Marguerite's. She liked things the way she liked them. I reached down into the wood box beside the stove.

"No. Not that one. Merde, it'll burn forever and it's too hot today for that. And we don't need more smoke in the air for nothing, do we?"

The spread-out fingers of my hand waited.

"Take the piece beside it. The birch."

I got the fire going in the stove and when the kettle had boiled long enough to please her, I made tea. Regular for me, calming tea for her in her favorite cup that she always kept on the stove's upper shelf. When I placed the cup on the table in front of her, she asked, "What's so funny?"

I hadn't realized I'd been smiling. I shared my thought with her. "If it hadn't been for you and your garden and the many things you get them to bring you from Boston, I wouldn't be able to make you this special lemon balm tea, would I?"

"I guess not. It's remarkable how God takes care of us, isn't it?" She leaned over the cup and closing her eyes, breathed in deeply through her nose. "And I am more than grateful for that. And to you, too, my dear girl. What would we ever do without you around here?"

"You would manage, I'm sure. Have I not trained Gig's woman well enough to help people when I'm not here? And my own Su'n has learned much now that she has settled down with her husband."

"Don't forget Rabbit Woman. She is still able to help with many illnesses. And Geneviève when she decides to show up."

"So they are. And now, Marguerite, after you have taken our conversation about your nightmares for a walk, why don't you bring it back here and tell me more about your... How do you say nightmare in French?"

"Cauchemar. Un cauchemar. Deux cauchemars."

"Tell me about them."

"I don't know if I can."

"Try."

She sipped her tea. "It's good, Keskoua. Good tea. Thank you."

"Stop trying to change the conversation."

"Very well." She set her cup down, adjusted her skirt, then looked into my eyes. "It's always that I can't find him. And I can't even feel him. It's like he's gone. Dead. I—"

A noise at the entrance of the cabin made both of us jump.

Several children, eyes large and full of fear, fidgeted in Marguerite's doorway. Two of them were my nephews, Gi´gwesu's sons.

"We have to talk to you, Keskoua. Come outside."

I did.

"You found J-B? Is he na to´q?" I asked them. "Marguerite told me you were helping her look for him."

"We were, Keskoua. So were Tata´t and Giju´, Papa and Mama. We were just there. At the fort. You have to come back. You have to go away."

"Go back? Go away? What are you saying? Where? Who told you that?"

Gig's younger son pushed past me and entered the cabin. I could hear his and Marguerite's voices. They were whispering.

"You have to go with the Chief," Snowy Owl, Gig's elder son said.

"You have to go with Singing Bear. To Big Meadow. Right away. They need you." He was very grown up for his ten winters so his face was serious, stern and worried all at the same time.

Wasueg, Gi´gwesu's woman, rushed in now, the baby in her belly not yet big enough to slow her down. "It's true. Singing Bear is already waiting for you at the docks. He knows all about it."

"Is this some kind of trick? Singing Bear told me nothing of this."

My brother, carrying their two-year-old daughter pick-pack, said, "Really, Keskoua? I would have thought you'd be the first to know." Gi´gwesu's grin told me not to ask, but I did anyway.

"What is that supposed to mean? How would I know the business of Singing Bear? He does not confide in me."

Wasueg smiled. "That's not what we heard."

Full of seriousness, Snowy Owl spoke again. "That bâtard Benny Church has kill—"

"Hush!" Wasueg could barely control the smile that threatened to make her admonishment to Snowy Owl ineffective.

"Mesgei, Giju´, I am sorry, Mother. But that bad, bad man has killed one of the healers in Big Meadow and taken another one away. They were asking a prisoner and he told them everything. Keskoua must go with Lnu Saqamaw to help them."

"They burned down their houses and killed their cows and chickens, too," said Gig.

"How do you know all this?"

"The prisoner wasn't a New Englander. He is one of us, an Acadian who masqueraded as one of them."

"Ah."

"And before he left, J-B found a dead pigeon with more information on its leg."

"A pigeon? From Boston?"

"Mesgei, moqwa´, sorry, no. It came from Big Meadow. They won't let anyone leave. They are starving to death there."

How could this be? How could even the New Englanders treat people like this? "Na to´q. I will go."

Behind me, Snowy Owl's little brother held out his arm. My munti swung from his small fist. He had not yet been named by the Grandfathers and Grandmothers, but we all called him Mouse.

Then from the other side of me, at the end of Wasueg's arm swung another bag, this one no doubt containing requirements for traveling. "You'll need this, too."

From behind Mouse, her eyes ready to spill water, Marguerite appeared out of the cabin door. She held her hands together like she was saying a prayer. "What is this I hear? What about J-B?"

"But the tide won't be going out for quite some time," I said. "What's the hurry?"

Wasueg came up close to me and whispered, "You aren't going by ship. You are going overland. With Bear and with Pierre Poitou."

I grunted a complaint.

"At least you'll have a—what do they call them? Hah. A chaperone." She giggled.

"There's nothing funny about this situation. Where is my son?"

I took my munti from Mouse and slung it over me. "Thanks."

"Na to´q."

I reached for the traveling bag that Wasueg was still holding out to me. I said nothing, but I think Wasueg knew I would be happy to have a chaperone.

"Where is my son?" Marguerite grasped Snowy Owl's wrist. "What do you mean 'Before he left'? He left? Left where?"

Gig and Wasueg exchanged glances.

"What do you know of this?" Marguerite's face had turned the color of a masgwi, a white birch tree. "Tell me."

Snowy Owl spoke before his father or mother could. "You didn't know? He found out where Second Son and Falcon disappeared to. He went after them."

Marguerite grabbed Snowy Owl's shoulders but before she could shake him, Gig stepped in to separate them. "Your son is an intelligent man, Marguerite. He knows the way of the bush. He knows the land between here and Big Meadow. Try to trust that knowledge in yourself."

"Merde." Marguerite whirled away toward the back yard. "CLAUDE! *Nous avons un problème!*"

Four

The trip overland from Port Royal to Mtaban near Big Meadow should have taken no more than four or five days, but because our young soldier, Pierre Poitou, was inexperienced with the bush, it took us longer.

We hadn't gone much farther than a mui´n, a bear, would travel in a day, before I asked Singing Bear why we had not gone by sea.

"No captain, not even KrommeZee, would risk it. Perhaps especially KrommeZee."

"How do you know Captain KrommeZee?" asked Pierre, his manner telling me he had not been sent along with us to study plants and collect leaves and berries.

"Who does not know Captain KrommeZee?" Bear said this before I had even formed the reply in my own head. Bear even managed to sound innocent, something I had not yet mastered in myself. But I was trying, and I have to tell you I was getting better at it. And I had almost mastered the task of thinking about the words coming out of my mouth before they escaped. Almost.

Pierre's response told me *for certain* he was not with us to study plants or collect berries. He was not along with us as chaperone, either. Although I already knew that. He would be expected to give a full report of the destruction of Big Meadow when he got back to the fort. I smiled to myself thinking he would be the slowest message pigeon anyone had ever seen. No. He was with us for several reasons. Some reasons secret from us.

"How do *you* know Captain KrommeZee?" I asked, trying to act like I didn't know something was going on. I'm not sure I did a good job of it because he looked at me from the corner of his eye and made no attempt to answer me. He spoke to Bear.

"I heard…" Pierre began, "that Captain KrommeZee does more than build fast ships and test them out by delivering wheat and maple syrup to Boston. And I've heard he brings more than wool and tea back with him. What do you think, Chief Bear?"

"Oh?"

"What have you heard?"

"Who is going to tell a bunch of Indians anything?"

Pierre's mouth opened like a baby gapjagwej's about to accept a worm from his robin mother. He sputtered an apology. "What are you saying? Do you really think I am like *them*?" Pierre's face told me Bear's words had hurt him.

"I think it's time to stop for a break," I said. "Those boots of yours are not suited for walking along trails through the bush."

Pierre had his bottom on a rock before I had removed my munti from my shoulder.

"She's right, you know. Your boots might be good for keeping buckshot out of your toes, but they are not good for walking over uneven ground."

I opened my second bag.

"I have to get these off."

Bear stepped forward ready to warn him not to do that, but I said, "Let him. Look what I have." I waved a pair of strong walking moccasins at them.

"Are you sure they'll fit me?" With a sigh like what comes before a storm, he pulled his boots off and reached for the moccasins.

"Just try them. I think you'll find them many times more comfortable than those things." One of his socks already had a hole at the heel. "Socks off, too."

He removed both socks, tucked them into each other and slid the small bundle into one of his boots.

"Wait." I opened my munti. "I have salve to put on your heel first."

He made eye contact with me for the first time since we'd left the fort. "Thank you." He turned his face away as I applied the salve.

I laughed. "You were expecting this to hurt?"

Bear leaned down to tell him in a false whisper, "Keskoua carries medicines for both adults and babies."

Pierre grumbled. I could see his face getting red.

Still laughing, I said, "You need not worry. This one is for babies." I closed the package and put it back in my munti. "Monsieur Coté is often asked by your uncle to put the one for adults on prisoners while they are torturing them for information."

I couldn't help myself, and obviously, Bear couldn't either because we both held our stomachs with laughter.

"You realize that's not true, don't you?"

Shaking his head and still laughing, Bear said, "Don't tell him that. We'll have no control over him at all then."

After a brief rest, we continued toward Mtaban. I tried my best not to let it show that I was very proud of my friend Chief Singing Bear for the way he had changed the subject from Captain KrommeZee's many secret occupations to somewhere else. Captain KrommeZee was not only involved in bringing information about our enemies, the New Englanders, to the fort and to our people and the French, but he was still involved with helping freed slaves come to our land where they could live their own lives among us. He built his fast ships near Big Meadow, and we all hoped the New Englanders had not yet discovered exactly where. But what we hope does not always come to be.

Five

I must tell you that I came to admire the young soldier, Pierre Poitou, before too long. He respected us, so respected our ideas and that made the journey less difficult for all of us. We were able to stop worrying about Pierre's feet, but now we had to face something that made each step more difficult.

I found a dead pigeon. Like all the others we had found, it had been shot.

I had stepped off the trail to relieve myself and noticed the empty pile of feathers and the little piece of paper still wrapped around one leg. With as much respect as I could manage, I removed the message but did not read it. I brought it back out to the path and handed it to Bear.

"What's this? Oh."

He spread the tiny piece of paper open and read: "We need your help. They're killing all our cows and chickens. Smoke everywhere. Dangerous. Some of us were injured. One healer is dead and they took the other one with them. Bastards! We need help. Healers. Please. Can you afford to spare one of yours? They are keeping us here."

"That's not exactly news, is it?" I said.

"No, it isn't. Here." He handed the message to Pierre. "Take care of this."

Pierre took it with finger and thumb barely touching it. He held it like that for several moments before he slid it into a pouch at his waist.

Bear looked up through the heavy canopy of trees then suggested we camp for the night.

I did not argue.

***

When I was a young girl, my friend Claude Guidry told me many stories about his life in the land called France. He told me of their strange ways, and of the dangers of being a king if you happened to have a younger brother—or even a cousin or uncle—who wanted to be king. When I remembered his stories, I wasn't surprised to learn that some people, whether they wanted to be king or not, would do almost anything to get what they wanted from somebody else.

I don't know if it was because Pierre was tired from walking, if he was starting to trust me, or if it was because of the little bottle he had in one of his pockets and drank from, it seemed, every time the wind caressed the trees around us, but he began to talk.

We had not dared build a fire that evening, so we had our bearskin blankets wrapped tightly around us. Buried in his own blanket, Bear made rumbling noises behind us as he slept.

"We call those people two-spirited," I told Pierre. "Our people, the Mi'gmaq, accept them."

Pierre's eyes got bigger. "You can't be serious. No one accepts those sinful creatures. It's against God's law. Pure and simple."

"Unless you're a king?" I tried to hide my smile without much luck. "Or someone who writes the music for ballets?"

"That's different." Pierre took another sip from his little bottle.

"Different how? And what are you going to do when you run out of whatever is in that bottle?"

Pierre reached inside his bearskin blanket and produced another small bottle. "And they'll have more where we're going, right?" Thumb and finger on the bottle's neck, he wiggled it.

I uncrossed my legs and re-crossed them the other way and adjusted my blanket around me better.

"Well?"

"Well yourself. My friend Claude—I believe you know him?—told me about Louis and Lully. How did they get away with it and you could not?"

Now Pierre's eyes narrowed. "Some people have money. Some people have power. Those with both money and power can more easily keep secrets." Pierre drained the last bit of what I knew was some kind of liquor from his bottle. With great care, he replaced the cap and slid it back inside his bearskin blanket and drew out the other one again. "They will have more there, won't they?"

Normally, a childish frown like the one Pierre now had on his face would have had me concerned if he had been a child, but he was not. He was, perhaps twenty-four or twenty-five winters old. I said nothing. Instead, I rose to my feet. "I think it's time to waken Bear. I need to sleep."

"Won't they?"

I didn't dare speak a word to this young man even though I wanted to scream at him, asking if he had ever, in his entire privileged life, had the misfortune to see what happened to people who had had no food, water, shelter or even clean air to breathe for more than a week. Instead, I shook Bear awake.

"Already? Let me go back to my dream, Keskoua. At least, until I get to kiss you in it. You were about to let me do that."

Again, I had to restrain myself from saying anything.

Bear rose from the ground and walked away behind some trees.

I adjusted the cedars he had been lying on and shook out my own bearskin blanket. I lay down and covered myself with it and used my munti as a pillow.

I heard Bear returning to where Pierre was sitting. "I suppose she talked your ear off," he said, and he laughed.

"I kept asking her about something, but she wouldn't answer me. Is she always that rude?"

I heard the rustle of Bear's deerskin leg coverings as he sat. "What do you want to know?"

"I merely asked her if there would be a chance to refill this."

"Lie down and get some sleep, Pierre. You're going to need it."

"But—"

"Do not make me repeat myself."

A further rustle of clothing and bearskin told me that Pierre had done what he was told. Perhaps he was a child after all. All Bear and I needed. We had enough dangers ahead of us without having to worry about a little baby in our care.

Six

I awoke to Bear's voice informing me he had made break-fast tea. I looked upwards, expecting to see clouds, but stars still twinkled faintly above the trees. It was morning, yes, but only just. Sun was barely lighting the sky.

"Careful, it's hot." He handed me a birch bark cup. "I sent our young friend on ahead."

"App?"

"I said I sent—"

"I know what you said, but why did you do that? In the dark? He has no experience with the bush in daylight, how will he ever manage…?"

Bear held out his hand to help me rise to my feet, but I ignored it and managed on my own. Without spilling my tea. Or grunting.

"He'll be fine," Bear said. "I told him to go only as far as the big white rock and wait there. And I told him to make note of everything he saw and to watch for dead pigeons without stepping off the trail."

"And you really think he's going to listen to you."

I really liked Bear's laugh. "Oh, he'll stay on the trail all right. I told him some stories before he left."

Although the tea smelled wonderful and I was thirsty after a night of sleeping deeply, I handed my cup back to Bear. "I'll be right back." I needed to relieve myself.

By the time I returned to our sleeping area, Bear had both our bearskin blankets tied in a bundle on his back. My cup was in his outstretched hand. "Don't forget your munti."

"Don't ever worry about me and my munti. It has become part of my body." I slung it over my shoulder before I took a sip of tea. It was very good. "You make good tea," I told him as I fell into step behind him. "So what's the real reason you sent Pierre on ahead?"

"I didn't give you an un-real reason yet."

"You know what I mean."

The bush was quiet, not even the birds or animals were awake. But I wanted to think they were waiting for Bear to answer my question, too.

Bear took his eyes off the path to turn his head back toward me. "I heard the beginning of Pierre's conversation with you last night before I fell asleep." He turned his face away again. "I want to hear the rest of it."

"At what point exactly did you fall asleep?"

"Start at the beginning anyway."

So I did.

"Pierre's family was a wealthy one. One of the wealthiest in France, he said. They were friends with the king and had some influence over decisions made by the king.

"You know, of course, that Claude Guidry knows all about what happens in wealthy families in France."

Bear nodded.

"Claude has told me many things and one of them is that the oldest male child inherits everything, so the oldest male child has his choice of almost any woman as a wife and any occupation."

"So far you haven't told me anything I don't already know."

"He always laughs about this because he says if you're that rich, you don't need an occupation. I recommend you don't get him talking about this because he'll start grumbling and complaining that this is why he ended up walking traplines in the bush instead of living the life of luxury in la Place des Conquêtes like his oldest brother does."

"Keskoua, I know all that. We're talking about Pierre now? And we don't have much time. We'll soon be at the big white rock. I didn't dare send him far. I know the dangers of the dark as well as you. Keep talking. And about Pierre, not about your 'friend' Claude Guidry."

My mouth opened, ready to remind my Chief that Claude and I were nothing more than friends and had never been and that he should stop spreading the old women's rumors like that, but I shut it again. Sometimes, I was just as guilty as Claude was when it came to talking. I could go off track like an atu'tuej, a squirrel, climbing a tree. They never went straight up or even all at once. This picture in my head made me laugh thinking that the old women's rumors wandered everywhere, too.

"I heard that. What's so funny?"

"Nothing you would understand."

Bear's grunt of disapproval made me laugh even louder.

"Na to´q, na to´q. All right, all right, I'll continue. Sometimes, you can be so serious, Bear."

"You don't give me the information I need, I'll show you serious." I didn't need to see Bear's face to know that he was hiding a smile while trying his best to look stern.

I continued. "Pierre's father, also named Pierre, was the oldest boy in his family as his father had been. But Pierre's father's first three children were female, and Pierre's father's wife was older than he was, and getting older, so he was worried that he would never have an heir to the family fortune. And name. Names are important to the wealthy and powerful, too. Did you know that?"

Bear didn't respond.

I couldn't help it. I added another little bit of information. "Did you know that the oldest daughter of Pierre's father's father is Gabbie Grenier's mother?"

"Keskoua."

"Just in case you wanted to know the connection between them, eʹe, yes? To Pierre, Gabbie is Uncle Gabbie. I think that's really nice. You know, to have family close by when you are so far away from your home. But I guess, because they're French, it would be mon oncle Gabbie?"

"Welaʹlin, thank you, Keskoua." He turned his head back to me. "But please, keep your feet on the same path until we get to the end of Pierre's story."

Right then, he tripped over a tree root and I did not keep my laughter inside me. "Look who's talking."

Bear turned back to the path so I could not see what his face looked like, but I could tell by his high, tight shoulders that there would have been a storm in his eyes.

"Pierre's father was concerned that he would never have a son but then along came a male child—Pierre. But less than a year after Pierre's birth, a second strong, healthy son was born. Pierre's father could finally be somewhat at peace. If something happened to the elder son, there was another ready to take his place. To inherit the state and to carry on the family name. A frequent happening, Claude told me, was that first sons often met with disaster. Oh, mesgei, sorry. I'm not supposed to mention my 'friend,' am I?"

"No… you're not…" Bear stopped walking and turned to me again. "Wait. In less than a year there was another child? How can that be?"

"I'm not sure I should share an age-old woman's secret with you, Chief Singing Bear. What if you tell the others?"

"Keskoua!"

"The wealthy have servants. Servants who perform all manner of duties for their masters."

Bear's laughter almost shook the trees. "Let me guess. One of two things. The father had a second wife, like the people in the north do. Or, the wife had a second husband who was…"—more laughter—"… who was less enthusiastic about spilling his seed several times a day trying to make a son, thereby weakening the supply?"

"You really don't know?"

Bear's shoulders moved upwards. "Tell me."

"Why should I? What will I get in return?"

I was trying to make a joke but Bear's eyes became softer than I'd ever seen them.

Before he could answer me—and I knew it would be with something I did not want to hear said, right then, at least—I added. "Never mind. I'll tell you."

His eyes shifted away from mine. Did I see disappointment in them? "Tell me."

"In the books I've read, the ones Marguerite gives me, I have seen the phrase 'wet nurse.' It means—"

Bear interrupted me. "I know this term." He turned back to the path again. "I understand now. Wealthy women have servants to nurse their children for them."

"When a woman is nursing her child, she does not easily become…"

Then we said this part together: "… with child."

"Interesting," said Bear. "So the wealthy and privileged and powerful end up with twice more children—"

"Than their servants."

"Is it true also what I heard," asked Bear, "that these wet nurses are nursing their own babies while they nurse the children of their masters?"

"Yes. But it's not necessary to have a baby to be able to produce milk. Can we not talk about this anymore?"

"Why? I find it interesting."

"My breasts are starting to hurt."

"Oh. Mesgei."

"This son—named Luc—was less than one year younger than Pierre and by the time they were of age, he had fallen in love with Pierre's betrothed."

"Betrothed?"

"The one promised to him. For marriage."

"I have heard that these promises are… What's the word? Ah. These promises are binding."

"Yes. Especially among the rich and the powerful. Like Pierre's family. And Pierre's betrothed… ah, what is the word he used for what she did? She 'reciprocated' the feelings of Pierre's younger brother. Is that how you say that word? Reciprocated?"

"I guess so," said Bear. "It means to do the same thing back, doesn't it?"

"E´e, I think so. I guess I said it right, then." I didn't wait again for Bear to tell me to keep talking. "The young woman was an only child and she was also from a wealthy family. Her parents were friends of Pierre's parents, so everybody got together and decided that a union of their families would be a union of both wealth and power, so they declared a betrothal between her and Pierre.

"Pierre said he was happy about this because she was very beautiful and kind, and also intelligent. And how did he say it? Oh, yes. He said, 'And having that much money coming to her didn't hurt either.' Do these people not consider love for each other? Or does this come later?"

"We're almost there."

"Na to´q. I'll say it fast. Pierre said that the young woman and his brother conspired together. They came up with what Pierre called 'a brilliant concoction of pure, absolute merde' to destroy his reputation and thus his life. They began to spread rumors that Pierre was not attracted to women. That he was often seen in certain areas of the city. In the company of effeminate men."

"Pierre is two-spirited?" asked Bear. "I would not have thought that. But why would that matter to anyone?"

"I don't understand it either."

"Wait. I think I know. The people from away want children to carry on their name and their property. Their property is very important to them. It's more important than... Than anything. Is this what you have learned? Is this what Claude told you?"

"Having someone take care of the family property and carry on the name is everything to them. But more than that, what they said about Pierre, would bring a terrible disgrace upon the name of the family. Pierre called it a 'black mark' against the family. I think that's what he called it."

The scolding voice of an atu'tuej in a tree above startled me. The four-legged ones were waking up. I stumbled against Bear.

Bear caught my elbow. "Na to´q, oqoti? Are you all right, dearest?"

No, I didn't miss the word he used, I pretended I didn't hear it even though the sound of it made my heart beat faster.

"I'm fine. I tripped." I turned my face away from Bear so he couldn't see the feelings trying to hide behind it.

He released my elbow. "Are you telling me, then, that Pierre lost his position as the firstborn son only because of these stories about him?"

"E´e. The shame on the family decided it."

"The more I learn about the Newcomers, the more confused I am."

"You are not alone. Watch where you're going. Stop staring at me. I'm fine."

Bear once more concentrated on the path ahead of us and we walked in silence for several moments.

Then Bear stopped. He turned to face me. "Let's not speak of this again."

I nodded agreement.

"Because I understand what it's like to love a woman who prefers someone else to me."

I tried to hold back from showing my thoughts, but I don't think I did it very well.

"And one more thing," Bear said.

I nodded agreement again.

"You snore, you know."

"I do not."

"And how would you know? That's the one thing not even you can do. Stay awake and sleep at the same time."

I pointed past his shoulder with my chin. "We're here. There's Pierre."

Seven

"I went farther than you said and came back." Pierre's proud smile and puffed-out chest told me he had something else to say. "It got light enough to see better."

Bear shook his head and teasing, glanced over at me. "Do these young people not know what happens if you are alone in the bush and run into a chenoo?"

I was still watching Pierre's face, so I saw his eyes react. Many of the Newcomers believed in our ways, but not in all of our ways.

"I've heard of the chenoo and it doesn't scare me one bit because there's no such thing."

I think what I admired most about Pierre was his openness. I wanted to believe I was the same way, but I wasn't. Pierre thought about things before they came out of his mouth, not like me, who thought about them after everybody else had heard them and had reacted.

Pierre's lips closed tightly and the corners turned down. "I believe in the Devil though. And his followers." He turned slightly to point farther down the path. "They are waiting for us down there. They're hiding in the trees. I heard them moving." His voice went quiet and he leaned over toward Bear and me. "I didn't get close enough to actually *see* them."

I believed him but I jumped anyway when a harsh voice came from inside the trees.

"Arrêtez où vous êtes, maudits. Stop where you are, damned people."

My breath came out of me and my shoulders went down at hearing French words instead of English ones.

Three men and three women stepped onto the path behind Pierre. They held muskets and knives, one held a sword, and one of the women, a tall, thin, wide-shouldered, fierce-seeming one, held a hoe. The woman with the hoe was one of our people; her hair was unbraided, signifying she was not married. She looked to be about thirty winters old. The other two women were short and plump, and although they had Acadian features, their skin was the color of mine. The two men would pass as either Acadian or Mi´gmaw, too. The third man was one of our people. They all had dirty faces and clothing, and their cheeks, even those of the plump women, were sunken.

Pierre stepped in front of me to face them. "Comment osez-vous nous parler comme ça. Qui pensez vous être? How dare you speak to us like that. Who do you think you are?"

I could not see Pierre's eyes but I could see the eyes of the woman with the hoe and I knew they were looking into his with interest. Yes. Pierre was a handsome man. Tall and strong. I knew why she would be attracted to him. Any woman would be.

Bear stepped forward then and spoke back and forth between our language and French. "I am Singing Bear. We come from Port Royal. I am Lnu Saqamaw, Chief, of our people. The woman is our healer. I don't know you people. Where is your Chief?"

No one answered. They did not move or change their faces.

Pierre moved back to stand beside me.

Bear continued. "We have received no pigeon messages from this area for many days, and the ones we did find contained such frightening information, we came to help. This man is a soldier from the fort." He turned and raised his hand to tell them he meant Pierre. This is when Bear looked into Pierre's face. If you can imagine the tail of a squirrel wanting to twitch but the squirrel itself didn't want it to, that's what Bear's eyebrows did at me.

What was he trying to tell me? I didn't want to make everyone look at Pierre if I did, so I kept looking ahead. I think I did it right.

"He is with us to collect information and bring it back to the men at the fort so they may plan strategies to assist you."

"A soldier, hein?" said the woman with the hoe, her voice deep and masculine, but tired. "Is this why he treats us with such disrespect?" The rising corner on one side of her mouth proved she was not about to slice the top of Pierre's head off with her hoe. This time I did look at Pierre and saw the same smile on his face.

Would Pierre's broken heart at last be soothed?

Pierre opened his mouth to say something but she spoke first. "I am Flower Stalk."

I could see redness crawling up Pierre's neck so I spoke to her to save him from getting redder.

I bowed my head. "I am Keskoua, the healer in my village. I am also the storyteller. I, too, come to collect information. But for a different reason."

"It is an honor." She bowed back to me, but kept her eyes on Pierre.

"His name is Pierre," I told her.

"Pierre."

One of the Acadian men, the lighter-skinned of the two, helped Bear remove the bearskin blankets from his shoulders. He hoisted them onto his own, handing his sword to the older Acadian woman.

"How far are we from Mtaban?" Bear asked him.

"Not far," said Flower Stalk before the man could answer. "Come with us."

"Aren't you going to search them," asked the other Acadian man who was dark skinned, hunched and wrinkled.

Flower Stalk ran her eyes from the top of Pierre's head down to his new moccasins and back up. "Maybe later."

***

By now, Sun was drawing shorter shadows from the bases of the trees we were walking through as we followed Flower Stalk into an unknown area. Here, guaq, pine trees, stretched up with nothing but their hats on. There were no paths, the ground was flat and smooth and covered with pine needles. We weaved our way, side by side, through them until an unbearable stench made my throat jump. Beside me, Pierre leaned over and threw the contents of his stomach onto the ground.

Wiping his mouth with his sleeve, he looked at me with sad eyes. "Sorry. It's just—" He leaned over and more liquid came up. "That smell."

"We're used to it by now," said Flower Stalk. "But it took a while. A long while. And even then, if the wind comes in just so…"

My own stomach finally reacted and my break-fast tea came out of my mouth onto the ground. "What is that smell?"

"You'll soon see."

We came out of the guaq onto a broad, muddy, brown beach that stretched almost as far as the low hills on the other side of the bay. Overhead, gulls circled screaming, their voices sounding angry and sad the same time. Everywhere lay the bloated bodies of humans, animals and even fish. Several trees along the edge of the guaq were fire blackened and leaning over, their backs broken. Overhead, the sky was cloudy with the smoke of burning, to the left and right of us.

I was unable to speak.

"This is beyond warring, isn't it?" said Flower Stalk, her eyes sad and her chin held firm. "They hate them, so they hate us, too, and everything about us."

The younger Acadian man swung our bearskin blankets from his shoulders and gently placed the bundle on the ground near a wikuom tucked in among large boulders and rocks. It was draped with seaweed and driftwood, I assumed to make it look like a boulder itself so invisible from the bay.

"It's us they're after," he said. "Acadians. Catholics. French. To them, we are all devils. And I am saying *real* devils. Everyone who is not one of them is a devil. Ask anyone who has had any dealings with them. Just ask *him*."

The older Acadian man grunted.

Flower Stalk pointed to another spot among the rocks where a second wikuom lay disguised. "We have only two wikuoms, I am sorry. It will be crowded sleeping but as you can see, we have no choice."

"And devils need to be destroyed. Have you heard what they do if they catch one of us alive?"

Flower Stalk turned to the younger Acadian man. "I know it's difficult for you, Lazare, but we have work to do. Try not to think about it right now. Later." She leaned toward me to say, "They took his wife and daughter alive." To Bear, she said, "We will eat if you are able to after the work that lies ahead. We'll make tea and pass the Talking Stick. I believe we have much to share with each other. Do we not?"

Pierre reached inside his jacket but before he had a chance to grasp his little bottle and bring it out, I was able to stop him.

"What!" he whispered, his eyebrows telling me he was annoyed. "No harm in asking, is there? Listening to them and looking at all this, I'm going to be needing more than the drop I have left as the day wears on. Yes?"

"No."

Bear stepped forward to hide the conversation between Pierre and me. "What can we do to assist you?"

The Mi´gmaw man pointed at the beach. "It is unpleasant work, but it must be done." His eyes met mine, then Pierre's, and came back to rest on Bear's. "Until the tide comes in, we go out there and bring in the bodies."

Pierre moved in close to me, like a child hiding in his mother's skirt.

"But there are dozens of them from what I can see. Where will we put them all?" He turned his face toward the guaq, but whispered to me, "None of your special healing teas will take the edge off *this* chore. I need to fill my bottle."

From the side of my mouth I said, "If you need something to comfort you, I have a sugar teat in my munti."

The Mi´gmaw man—his name was Otter—turned away toward the beach. "It must be done."

Flower Stalk explained, "Others come and take the bodies away from here once we bring them in. It creates less attention if we perform these duties in brief episodes. And it is more tolerable if these duties are shared. It's hard work. The others bury the dead when and where they can along the way back to their own village. They bury them at any place there's a soft spot they can dig into. They cover them with earth, seaweed and dead branches." She looked at me. "This is not our way, to bury our people just anywhere, but we have no choice."

"I understand," I said. "Like Bear said, what can we do?"

Flower Stalk motioned with her arm hooked that I should follow her, so we went into the guaq to a pile of foul-smelling clothing and blankets.

"We have no choice. This is all we have to transport them from there to here. I'm sorry."

"You said people come to take them away?"

"E´e. Some of them are people from your village. How do you not know this?"

Eight

We had moved twenty-four dead people from the beach to inside the trees before the dark, dirty seawater began to lick at my moccasins.

Flower Stalk put her arm out to stop me from going back in. "That's all we can do for now. When the tide comes in, so do their patrol boats. We cannot let ourselves be seen. We have been lucky. They have not yet discovered this place." She took a corner of the blanket Pierre was using and helped him pull it toward the guaq.

"What will happen if they find us?" Pierre asked, as he, with great respect, rolled the small body off the blanket onto the floor of the guaq bush. "This one is a mere child. How can they do this to children? How can they do this to anyone?"

"They hate us," said Flower Stalk with no emotion in her voice. "They hate them—you French, you Acadians—and they hate us. To them, we are all the same. We are all savages. We are not Protestant and that makes us heathens, savages, wild, brainless people, something to be burned at the stake and sent to their Hell."

"Not all of them are like that," Pierre said. "I have known some fine men who are Protestant and who hold nothing against the French."

"I have met good English men, too," said Otter as he and the younger Acadian woman—Francine was her name—dragged in the final body. "Even some good New Englanders."

The older Acadian man laughed. "I swear you must live in a fantasy world, Otter. There is no such thing as a good New Englander."

Otter smiled back at him. "You know what I meant."

"Not all of them hate us, Chief Flower Stalk," said Francine as she held the blanket out at full arm's length to fold it. "I know it must feel like that to you, and I've said it before, even to you—with all respect, of course—not all Maudits anglaises are maudits. Some of them hate each other and I feel sorry for the ones who are hated. Especially those burned at the stake." She shivered. "I can't imagine putting someone through that." She placed the blanket she had folded on top of the pile with the others. "And they say that their god wants them to do it."

Francine was speaking of things I was, sadly, already aware of, except that Flower Stalk was Chief. Where were the rest of her people?

I asked her.

"The rest of my people? This—" her hand swept the air from the beach to the trees, "is the rest of my people."

"You mean…?"

"Yes. As I said. They hate the French, they hate us. To them we are all the same." She folded Pierre's blanket then took mine from me and set them on the pile. "Let us wash up and have something to eat." She glanced at Pierre. "Will you be able to eat something? Are you feeling any better?"

"I'd feel a lot better if I could get my hands on a bottle of whiskey. Do you have anything like that hidden somewhere?"

Otter spoke up, "We barely have food, young man."

Pierre hung his head. "Sorry. I wasn't thinking. All of this is so overwhelming."

Without a word, Flower Stalk walked away to the beach where she crouched behind a large boulder to dip her hands into a pool of water that was collecting there. "Come. Wash up. It will help take our minds off all this."

I followed her.

"You mean to tell us that they killed all of your people except you and Otter?"

"And these two Acadian men and these two Acadian women. They are also family. We were close to five hundred people, all told. And now—" Her voice cracked. "Why?" She rose to her feet. "Come. Let us get something to eat and drink."

***

Before long, a small fire was heating water for tea and eight of us were seated cross-legged around it. The little bit of smoke coming from our fire joined with the dirty gray clouds above us. It would not be noticed by the patrol boats.

"Where's Otter?"

"On lookout," said Flower Stalk, making eye contact with each of us. "As we all must be. Keep part of your mind aware at all times while each of us speaks." From beside her leg, she drew out a small stick. "This is a far cry from being our sacred Talking Stick, but it will have to do. If they find this one, they will think nothing of it. We must not leave even the tiniest shred that we are still here."

"Good thinking," said Bear.

"And this…" she indicated the fire. "Is a far cry from being a sacred fire." Her smile was a weak one. "But it will have to do."

No one laughed.

"Is everyone comfortable speaking in French?"

An agreeing mumble went around the Circle but stopped at the second Acadian man, the older, wrinkled, hunched one, whose name I did not know. "I suppose," he said in English.

"I have a question," said Pierre, reaching inside his jacket.

I jabbed him with my elbow and through my teeth I whispered, "The answer is no and it will always be no."

"But how can we hold a meeting without something to take the edge off? Something to make us feel comfortable enough to talk?"

I pointed to his birchbark cup. "You have tea."

"Tea. And tea is supposed to help us say the truth about what is on our minds."

"Tea."

"Are we ready?" asked Flower Stalk. "Does everyone understand how the Talking Stick works?"

Another agreeing mumble went around the Circle, this time, stopping at Pierre.

"Ask your questions now. Once the Talking Stick starts around the Circle, no one may speak unless it's in his hand."

"Except if someone hears the enemy approach," added Bear, who received a respectful bow of Flower Stalk's head.

"Yes. Then you may speak. This would be an exception, oui? To allow for the special circumstances we find ourselves entwined in? As though we were a spider's next meal?"

"I wouldn't have put it quite like that," I said, trying to lighten the atmosphere but obviously failing at it because Flower Stalk's face turned sad and worried.

"French is not my mother tongue. Did I make a mistake in my grammar?"

"No. No. Not at all. And it's not mine either. I mean, I would not have put it that way because I am scared enough without making it worse by making me think about being eaten."

No one laughed.

"We shall begin with the person on my left. Gisèlle? Speak."

Before Flower Stalk handed the tiny stick to Gisèlle, the older Acadian woman, she added. "One more thing. Do not caress this poor wee stick too hard. It must continue to look like an ordinary stick. If the bark is picked off, or if it becomes smooth and shiny from rubbing—like our usual Talking Stick has become—it will be noticed. Hold it gently. It will still help you say what is deep inside."

Nodding agreement, Gisèlle wrapped her gnarled hands around the stick. Her sigh was deep. "I lost my husband and two grandsons to the fighting. And our farm was destroyed."

"What is the exact location of your farm?" Everyone's head turned toward Pierre. "Is it at… the shore… or … farther… inland?"

No one said a word.

"I need to know." He shrugged. "For my report. I need to know how badly each dike is affected."

Everyone continued to stare at him.

"Sorry."

Flower Stalk nodded to Gisèlle.

"This loss has affected me deeply."

"But what if I start paying attention to the wrong things? I was given many questions. What if I forget them?"

With great patience, Flower Stalk replied. "This is also a good exercise in remembering. But we must listen, too. Listen and remember everything each person says. Everything each person says. You will no doubt find your answers in their words. *If* you remain patient and pay attention to each of us."

"Isn't that your job, Keskoua? You're the storyteller, not me."

"It isn't about you," I said as quietly and with as much respect for the Sacred Circle as I could. It wasn't easy. I wanted to become a gu´gu´gwes, an owl, the kind that screeches. "It's about these people. These people are our family now. They are now us and we are they. Don't you understand?"

"All I understand is that my whiskey bottles are empty and I—"

Lazare said, "We're all afraid."

"Yes, we are," said Flower Stalk. "Please continue, Gisèlle."

Gisèlle looked down at her hands and I think she realized she had been twisting the Talking Stick because she said, "Ooh," and dropped it onto her lap. Quickly, she picked it up again to hold it against her chest.

Pierre muttered, "But I'm not afraid. I just want to take the edge off."

"Ta gueule."

"There's no need to be rude," he whispered back.

"Obviously there is. Now shut your trap."

Gisèlle spoke. "My heart is breaking. It will never heal. In all my years, and in all the years of my ancestors, there has never been talk of anything so vile." She turned to me. "Although I am mostly French, mostly Acadian that is, part of me is Mi´gmaw. I can trace my Acadian French ancestors back almost one hundred years. My other ancestors, my ancestors who came from this land, go back many years. Many, many generations."

"E´e," said Flower Stalk without making more than a breath of sound come out of her mouth.

Pierre leaned toward me and I knew it was to whisper a question, but I opened my eyes wide and squeezed my lips together. He settled back.

Gisèlle looked at each of us in turn. "Never. Never anything so vile."

With the Talking Stick now across both palms, she lowered her hands to rest against her crossed ankles. She stared down at it. "You could hear them. In the barn. They were... They were burning. My husband and I and my two grandsons went out of the house to help. We wanted to open the barn doors. So the animals could escape, you see?"

Several of us nodded.

"But the Maudits anglaises were hiding in the trees and shot at us. My husband told me to run back to our house. I obeyed him. I didn't want to, but... And then the Maudits anglaises shot my husband and both my grandsons. I saw it happen. I saw them fall. I saw them writhing in pain in the dirt."

Flower Stalk reached over to caress Gisèlle's knee. The man on my side of Gisèlle, the wrinkled old man who had spoken in English, did the same to the other knee.

"Do we ever get over seeing something like this?" I could tell that Gisèlle did not expect an answer. It wasn't really a question. It was a statement. "My daughter—the mother of these grandsons of mine—died twelve winters ago. A difficult birth. The baby did not survive either. I'm sure if my daughter had survived, seeing this would have broken her heart. Is it wrong to say it was a blessing that my daughter was already dead?"

I don't think Gisèlle expected an answer to this question either, but Flower Stalk shook her head. "Moqwa´, no."

A weak smile. "I could not go out to them. I could not help them. Help them? I knew they were gone. They were there. First standing. Then down on the ground. Moving. Struggling. Then nothing. And even when darkness came, and the Maudits anglaises went away, and I went out to move the bodies of my husband and grandsons, I could not help them. I was not strong enough. Even in my rage and grief, I was not strong enough. It was two days before someone passed by." She looked past the old man beside her to Lazare who was between me and him. "It was you. And I will be eternally grateful to you for your help." To me, she said: "He helped me bury them. Lazare helped me bury them."

Heads bowed toward Lazare.

"Thank you, Lazare. Thank you." Gisèlle handed the Talking Stick to the man who had spoken English.

The face of this man was like a clay field baked in the sun. His clothing was no dustier or dirtier than that of anyone else's, but it had a tiredness to it their clothing didn't. "I don't have a name," he began. "I didn't want to have one of theirs so they called me Dit Ça." In English he said, "It means Called That and that's what everybody calls me now." He glanced at me. "I'm not really certain, but I think I am about fifty-five winters old. But I know I was born in the summer so would that be fifty-five summers old?"

I didn't respond. I was very aware of how the Talking Stick works, and besides, he wasn't making a joke.

"You are ignoring me?"

I shook my head and looked at my feet at the end of my crossed legs.

"She's ignoring me!"

Flower Stalk spoke up. "She is not, Dit Ça. You hold the Talking Stick. Remember how that works? Only the person holding the Talking Stick can say anything. Unless you ask me, your Chief, a question that is important enough to you to ask me." The smile she showed to Gisèlle was small so extra kind.

The old man slumped back into his original curled shape that reminded me of a gopit, a beaver, curled over its own Talking Stick, ready to nibble on it. "I forget things."

Beside me, Lazare stretched out his arm to rub the shoulders of Dit Ça.

"I don't know which reason it is that I forget things." This he said first looking at me, then at Pierre, then at Bear, who was sitting beside Flower Stalk. "I am fifty-five winters—summers!—old so perhaps it is because my brain is old? But it wasn't old when I first came back here, was it? And I couldn't remember things then. I was thirteen summers old when the French got Acadia back from the Maudits anglaises. I must ask someone, please, what year was that?"

Still with his hand on Dit Ça's shoulder, Lazare leaned toward him to say, "That would have been in 1667. What do you remember about returning to your homeland?"

"I was afraid of the French. And especially the Indians."

"And you didn't know...? What didn't you know?"

"Ah, yes. Now I remember. Merci, Lazare. Thank you. I was afraid of the French and the Indians. That is very funny. I *am* French and Indian. Indian? Not Indian. I am not from India, I am from here. I am Mi´gmaw and French. I am Acadian. They took me away and taught me their ways. They made me hate my own ways. Fear my own ways."

"And?"

"Na t´oq, I am na t´oq. You aren't supposed to speak." Dit Ça waved the Talking Stick at Lazare. "See?" He laughed. "I hold it now. I am the only one who is permitted to speak. But thank you. For helping me through that. I remember where I'm going now."

With a final, gentle pat, Lazare removed his hand from Dit Ça's shoulders.

"They hit me a lot," Dit Ça said, pointing to his head. "The bruises don't show under your hair, eh? That's what somebody told me. Another boy who was there, too. This boy was eight years old. I was six and my friend was seven. They didn't hit her as often as they hit me, but they still did. That can make you forget things. It can hurt something inside even though your head is hard."

I guess he saw my raised eyebrows because he said, "Oh. *She* was Dit Ceci. It means Called This. And don't ask me why they used these names because I only *think* I know. But I think I'm right, too. But they knew how to pronounce these words. They would say them correctly. They would say, *dee saw* and *dee suh-see*. I don't understand why, if they knew our language, French, they didn't speak to us in French. Strange, isn't it?"

Flower Stalk nodded approval and her compassionate smile told him to continue.

"I think it was because I used to point to things, and so did Dit Ceci. We wanted to know in their language, so we would ask, 'Qu'est-ce que c'est que ça?' What's that? Or 'Qu'est-ce que c'est que ceci?' What's this? If they knew French, they didn't let us know, but I think they knew enough to call us those names. Instead of our real names."

He looked at the Talking Stick closely and reached out with finger and thumb at a piece of loose bark. Then, shaking his head, he pulled his hand back quick as a frog's tongue with a bug already in it. "No. Don't change it."

He looked at me again. "Do you want to hear more?"

I hoped my face told him yes.

"I don't know my real name. I don't remember. At all. Dit Ceci says she can't remember hers, either. They tell us though—the people here—that my father's name was Bernard and her father's name was Guillaume, but these names have no meaning for either of us. The name Marie is familiar to her for her mother's name. But—" His smile was happy and sad at the same time. "What Acadian woman does not have a Marie either in her own name or that of her mother or aunt or sister?"

He straightened the curve of his back. As much as he could anyway. "But you're not here to listen to me talk about my days in New England living with the Puritans as next thing to a slave, are you?"

"Slave?" came out of Pierre's mouth.

"Indentured servant," said Dit Ça. "Same thing when you take our ages into account. I heard it said that when the New Englanders first arrived, they tried to enslave the native people. Us. Well, I am part of us, am I not?" he asked Flower Stalk, who nodded. "The imported dark-skinned people were too costly, they said." His laugh was not a real laugh. "Didn't take long for us to die off. And it wasn't the physical strain. It was in the mind. And that's what I think happened to me. Because I was part of us and not so much of the French Newcomers here or the English Newcomers there. Maybe it wasn't being struck in the head so many times my memory got broken. It could have been that my will to stay alive in a cold barn with their animals damaged my mind. What do you think?"

No one responded to his question, but all of our eyes looked into his with sadness.

"How do the dark-skinned ones survive that?" He thrust the Talking Stick at Lazare. "Sorry. That's all I have to say this time. Sorry."

Before Lazare's hand closed around the Talking Stick, I thrust it back toward Dit Ça. Immediately, Lazare drew his hand back. He turned to me and nodded. His lips said, *I want to hear more, too.*

"You want me to keep talking, is that it?" I wasn't certain if Dit Ça was angry or pleased. He was difficult to read.

"Very well then." He once again reached toward a loose piece of bark on the Talking Stick and withdrew his hand.

"They told us our parents had been killed in the fighting. How would we know anything different? When we returned to our land, here, we learned that the New Englanders had not told us the truth. Our parents were alive when we were taken away. Their grief over losing us shortened their lives. We never saw them again and they never saw us again.

"I see a question on your face, Lazare. You wonder why the New Englanders wanted us."

Lazare nodded as did I and several others in the Circle.

"They felt sorry for us. They told us they were saving us from someone called Satan."

This time, I was the one who opened my mouth. "You mean it's not just the Priests who talk about that strange creature?" I immediately slapped my hand over my mouth.

Beside me, Pierre snickered.

"They are much worse," Dit Ça said. "The Priests tell us we are all going to Hell. Those people send us there in flames."

Several of us changed legs.

"The boy I told you about?" He turned to Bear. "The one who told me no bruises show up under the hair?"

Bear bowed his head.

"They burned him at the stake."

"No!" This exclamation from both Pierre and me.

"They had named this boy, Beelzebub."

A grunt from Lazare made me frown at this.

"Beelzebub is another name for Satan," Dit Ça explained. "This is how they thought of this boy in the first place. His name was Barthelemi and somehow they found that to be a great offence against their god."

This time, the bit of bark was plucked off the Talking Stick.

"I don't understand it except I know he refused to speak English although he was exceptionally good at it and helped me and Dit Ceci learn it. Without him, we would have been burned at the stake, too. We weren't the most obedient children when it came to adopting their ways. Or adapting to them, either."

I wondered how this man had survived such experiences.

Lazare was next but instead of speaking, he handed the Talking Stick to me.

"No, no. Take a turn. Talk to us. It's good to talk."

"What do you know about anything?"

"I'm a healer."

"She's a healer," said Pierre.

"Hush."

Flower Stalk said, "Talk, Lazare."

Where Dit Ça seemed to be full of a word I couldn't think of because maybe there is no word for it, but means full of emptiness—and I know that makes no sense but that's the way he seemed to me—Lazare was a frozen rock. If you put a frozen rock into any fire, not only a Sacred Fire, it can explode into tiny dangerous pieces.

"They took my wife and daughter. My daughter is twelve years old. I can't let myself even imagine what they might do to her. Or to my wife. But my daughter… She's only twelve."

Like Lazare had done for Dit Ça, I did for him: I rubbed his shoulders.

"When we heard them coming, my daughter—her name is Yvonne— ran out to save her lamb. It wasn't so much we heard *them*, we heard the screaming of animals from the neighbor's farm."

Gisèlle muttered a sound that meant she knew what that was like.

"And we saw the smoke. Her lamb was in the corral and she… she ran out. My wife and I ran out, too. Not for her lamb, even though we knew it was important to her, but for her. A man appeared out of the trees and pointed a pistol at me. I don't remember a lot after that." Lazare rubbed a spot on his head. "I was shot here. In the head. And another man shot me here, in the leg." He pointed at the bottom part of his leg.

A sympathetic whisper went around the Circle.

"I could see everything happening but could do nothing about it. I tried to get up but kept falling down. That's when the second man shot me, in the leg, you see." He pointed again. "They didn't shoot *them*. I saw them take them away." He turned to me. "Do you think they somehow heard she was our healer and that's why they took her away?"

My eyes went to Flower Stalk. Her shoulders went up and her head tipped to the side to tell me it was possible.

Lazare turned from me to Flower Stalk. "You said it could be."

"I did. And it could be."

"I heard from a friend in Boston that they want to take our healers and burn— I'm sorry." My hand went to cover my mouth so fast, it made my top lip smash into my teeth. It hurt.

"Na to´q, Keskoua. Don't ever think that thought of yours has not passed through my own mind. More than once. Day and night. Night and day." Lazare looked down at the Talking Stick. "I still blame myself even though I know I couldn't do anything. I tried and then… Well, I recall nothing except when the lamb came to nuzzle me in the face. That's what woke me up." He laughed. "You know what's funny? What's funny is that I feel just as angry at myself about not caring if the lamb lived." He shook his head. "I am filled with the most horrible guilt and anger about everything. Will it ever go away?" I think he expected—hoped for?—a positive answer, but no one said anything. He handed the Talking Stick to me.

"Finalement," Pierre gasped at me. "C'est le temps. It's about time. I can say something now?"

"Who is holding the Talking Stick?" I said, waving it in front of his face with as much respect for it as I could. "Who is holding the Talking Stick?"

"Well, you are, of course, but… It was between you there for… No?

Not yet?"

"Not yet. I don't have a lot to say so soon it will be your turn."

Pierre sighed and slumped back. He didn't even change legs. But I did.

"As you know, I am the storyteller and the healer from my village. My village is near Port Royal. We were asked to come here to help because we heard terrible stories from your pigeon messages. The messages that got through to us, that is. The Maudits anglaises were shooting them down. I don't like that term. Even though it suits them."

I laughed as did everyone else around the Circle except for the woman named Francine. She seemed lost in another world. A happy world. She was smiling, but not at what I had just said. People react to terrible situations differently. I would try to get her aside and speak with her if she wasn't able to speak using the Talking Stick when her turn came.

"I wasn't expecting to see such destruction."

Lazare patted my knee.

"I will do whatever I can to help. And the first thing will be to pass the Talking Stick along…" Here, I turned to Pierre and, hoping he caught what I was intending, I said, "… to get it quickly around the Circle so others can speak to perhaps relieve themselves of some of the pain in their hearts. Yes?"

Pierre's eyes rolled up at the sky as he flipped his hand out to me, palm up.

I placed the talking stick in his hand, but before I let go of it, I said, "Now it's about you, and nobody else but you." I let go.

As Pierre's hand closed around the Talking Stick, I heard a gasp rush into him. His eyebrows crashed together like a pair of fallen trees in a fast river in the spring. His lower jaw moved open slightly then shut.

"I…"

No one spoke. Gisèlle switched legs.

"I don't remember a thing about my First Communion, but I

remember my first Confession.

"I was highly stressed knowing I would have to stand in line with the other children, boys in my line, girls in the other—as though six-year-olds would have been having any thoughts that would include the Sixth Commandment." Pierre shook his head.

"I couldn't think of anything I could possibly have done against any of the other Commandments, let alone the Sixth. At that time at least." Pierre smiled at Lazare then closed one eye at Bear. "I couldn't think of a single thing I could have done that would constitute a sin to be confessed to whoever it was in that small, narrow, wooden box with its front curtain hiding him. The curtain-covered cubicles on either side of that small, narrow, wooden box were no less frightening. And this was only the practice run. We would be expected to shuffle ahead and individually, as each boy or girl exited, climb into that box and kneel." He shivered and moved the Talking Stick from one hand to the other and back again. "The real First Confession would be Saturday evening. This would give us less time to sin, I suppose, before Mass and our First Communion early Sunday morning. Our practice run involved nothing more than entering that dark space, kneeling, and waiting for whoever was inside to slide open a wooden window with wooden bars, say, 'In the Name of the Father, of the Son, and of the Holy Ghost,' while making the Sign of the Cross in tiny movements, then slamming the little wooden window closed again. This, although not stressful on its own, portended a problem.

"I had to think fast. I had to find a way to sin. It was already Friday, and I had chores to do for Papa. And I knew my mother would be wanting me to try on my First Communion uniform one more time, just in case a thread or a button were out of place.

"My home was neither a wikuom nor a cabin made of logs. The ships you have seen, and might cause you to imagine what *une grande maison* in my land would look like, would be a mere apartment in my home. I am saying this not to brag, but to help you understand how many people occupied my home. When growing up, I had an au pair. I don't know how to describe that to people who have no idea what that might be, but it would be like you, Keskoua, having a baby then immediately handing it over to someone else to raise."

I truly believe that if Pierre had known more about me, he would never have said such a hurtful thing. I had been forced as a young girl of only fifteen winters to do exactly that. My daughter Jeanne had been put inside me without my consent and my friend Claude and his wife, Marguerite, had taken her in for me and had raised her as one of their own.

Bear leaned forward with his elbows on his knees to shoot arrows out of his eyes at Pierre.

"Quoi? What?"

Bear leaned back into his original cross-legged position, his chin firm and his eyes distant and in slits.

"If I said something wrong, I'm sorry." Pierre looked at me with sadness in his eyes. "I know I'm missing something, but in all honesty, I do not know what it is. I'm sorry."

I patted Pierre's knee. "Na to´q."

Pierre turned to Flower Stalk. "What did I do wrong? What did I say?"

Flower Stalk bowed her head slightly and said, "Carry on. It is your turn to speak. Not hers."

Pierre slumped, curling into himself as though he were Dit Ça's mirror. The hand holding the Talking Stick moved toward Francine who was next in line.

"I said, carry on. It is your turn to speak, Pierre."

A deep intake of air seemed to uncurl Pierre and he wrapped both hands around the Talking Stick. "I could use a drink." His eyes darted at me then the air went out of him. "I went toward the dining area. I knew there would be many people in the food preparation rooms, and they would be very busy because mealtime would be within the hour. I was six years old. No one would notice me. I stood behind a young woman with her hair up in a net and an apron whose belt was barely long enough to make the required bow at her back. Her wide bottom would hide me from those on the other side of the long wooden preparation table. She was preparing green peas, splitting open the pods and thumbing the peas out into a small bowl. Occasionally, a pea would leap away onto the table from where she would snatch it up and pop it into her own mouth. All I had to do was wait. She was a chatty one, turning to her neighbors to the right and left of her often. And there it was.

"She had turned to the woman to the right of her and was saying, 'For the love of Jesus, I've never seen a man with one so large.' A single pea leaped from its pod onto the edge of the table. She hadn't noticed it yet. With thumb and forefinger, I snatched it from the table's edge and ran.

"I must tell you that I did not eat this pea. I threw it away. But now I had something to confess." He sighed. He smiled. "That felt good. I confessed the sin of stealing the pea, but I never confessed to anyone about stealing the pea for a devious purpose. Which I think would be a worse sin." Pierre laughed. "Yes. It feels really good. It feels really good. Here." He held the Talking Stick out to Francine. "Really good. But I still would like a drink of something."

"That's wonderful," said Francine, smiling widely with her mouth but not with her eyes as she took the Talking Stick from Pierre's hand. "I'm always so pleased when I hear stories with happy endings." She caressed the Talking Stick. "Like my story is going to end. They're going to come back. All of them. And soon. I just know it."

"I am reluctant to speak when you are holding the Talking Stick," said Flower Stalk. "But would you please say who is miss—"

"They are not missing. I just don't know where they are. They're going to come back."

"Just say who they are. There are three people in this Sacred Circle who know nothing of you or your family. Should you speak of someone they know nothing about?"

"Oh. Of course not. That would be rude." Francine nodded to me, then to Bear, then to Pierre. "My apologies. My husband, my two sons and my three grandchildren will be back. I know that Serena, the children's mother, is dead." Her eyebrows twitched for a moment as though she were trying to remember something. "They must have gone to look for a woman who can nurse the baby. The baby was born only a few days ago." She turned to me. "I know *she's* dead—the mother, I mean—because I'm the one who found her. I knew it was her because I know her so well. Knew her. Even though part of her face…"

Gisèlle struggled to her feet to cross around in front of Dit Ça, Lazare, me, then Pierre to squeeze in between Pierre and Francine.

"That has to be where they are. Right? Looking after the baby? I'm sure that's where they are. They'll be back." She smiled and nodding her head, she passed the stick over to Bear who didn't actually take it from her hand because she dropped it onto the ground between his crossed legs.

Bear snatched it up quickly and brushed it off even though I don't think it was on the ground long enough to have picked up any sand or salt or leaves.

"As you know, I am Chief of our village. I see the devastation wrought upon you, but I must advise, as will your own new Chief, I'm certain…" He nodded at Flower Stalk who bowed her head to him. "… not to let the Maudits anglaises kill our insides too. Some said I should have sent somebody instead of me in case something happened to me but what kind of a man would that make me? I am here to take care of Keskoua—"

"I'll bet you are," said Pierre. "In more ways than one, eh?"

All eyes turned to Pierre.

"Merde."

Bear continued. "Someone in my stead could not make that kind of decision about something so important. If I offer myself and my people to help you, I am responsible for their lives, not somebody in my stead."

Pierre nodded as did I.

"Like Pierre, and like Keskoua, I am here to learn and to offer help. But we must learn what to do." He handed the Talking Stick to Flower Stalk.

Flower Stalk remained silent for a moment. "As you can see, Sun is close to the bottom of the sky so we must extinguish our Sacred Fire lest they see it." She rose to her feet. "Someone please, go relieve Otter."

"Pierre. That's you."

"Yes, Bear. Of course." Pierre rose to his feet. He bent down to pick up his birch bark cup. "I'll just refill this." From the pot on the Sacred Fire, he poured water into his cup. "There, now. Where is he anyway?"

Every one of us pointed in the same direction. "Over there," said Dit Ça. "I will relieve you after I have a rest."

"I think we are all in need of rest," said Flower Stalk. "Men in that wikuom and ladies in that one."

At the edge of the trees, Pierre turned back. "Sleep well."

"That's the plan," Flower Stalk replied.

"And it's my turn to make sure those plans don't go awry." Pierre's back melted into the trees.

Nine

We slept. Men with men, women with women.

But before we slept, Flower Stalk, who was lying beside me in that crowded wikuom, propped her head up with her hand on her elbow and asked me, "Are you not afraid to be sleeping this close to someone with male appendages?"

"Ah. So now that sweet young Pierre is not within hearing distance, she is admitting to having spare parts. I thought perhaps you might have them. By your voice and certain mannerisms."

"Well, I wouldn't call them spare. They work just fine and I don't think I could manage certain bodily functions without them."

"Don't make me laugh."

"You have no problem with two-spirited people?"

"None. Why?"

"Although our people profess to accepting us, some have great fear when we are around them."

"I know this only too well from the mother of One-Eyed Joe. She's been gone for many years now, but she told me about two-spirited people whose lives were… What's wrong? You're making a strange face." I had seen a memory flutter across her eyes in the light of the waxing moon that poured in through the smoke hole above us.

"Was she a healer in your village?"

"Yes, she was. I learned everything I know from her. Well, from some other people, too, but mostly from her. Why?"

"When I was about eighteen winters old, we went to Port Royal. My mother and father and me. There was a woman there who said she learned many things from this woman, too, this mother of One-Eyed Joe. My mother and father had heard about her. This mother of One-Eyed Joe I mean. And about her healing methods. They heard she could maybe help me. I guess they didn't know she was dead. Well, actually, it wasn't my mother and father. They accepted me the way I was. It was the sister of the Chief who had a problem with me and had us sent there. Her son was my age. He was two-spirited, too. I think his mother wanted them to... What's the word? Experiment?"

I nodded.

"I think his mother wanted them to experiment on me first. And if it worked, she'd send her son. He and I were good friends. Too good in her mind, I think."

I must have smiled or something because she said, "Not that kind of friends. Real friends. We loved each other, but not that way."

"He was not attracted to you."

"No. I am womanly, remember? Two-spirited men are attracted to men, not women."

Flower Stalk lifted her head off her hand then lay back on the cedars beside me, staring up at the moon through the hole in the top of the wikuom.

"Do you want to talk about it?"

"That's exactly what she said."

"Who? The mother of One-Eyed Joe? Did you see her spirit?" This excited me as I had always hoped to see it, but never had.

Flower Stalk shifted again and turned to face me. "I've never seen anyone's spirit. That would be terrifying."

"I suppose it would depend on... on what they wanted to say to you."

Flower Stalk was back up on her elbow again, her voice a whisper. "You mean you believe those stories that the Fathers are always telling us? That their saints appear to people?"

"It's not like *those* stories. *We* see people we have known. Family. Good friends. Loved ones who have left for their Journey. They will sometimes try to help us."

"Do *you* see them? I'm not sure, even though it is our way, that I could ever believe in them."

"No," I told her with sadness. "Never. But I have seen messages from them. Signs that show they know I need help with something. These signs always make me think in another direction. So, no, I don't *see* them. They help *me* see."

I could tell she was thinking about that. Maybe trying to remember if she had received messages from her loved ones.

"You need to know that the mother of One-Eyed Joe didn't experiment on anybody. She helped two-spirited people but not in the way your friend's mother was thinking. Maybe hoping? The mother of One-Eyed Joe helped the two-spirited love themselves." I looked into her eyes. "Did the mother of One-Eyed Joe speak to you? Did you at least hear her voice?"

Flower Stalk closed her eyes as she shook her head, her smile kind. "It wasn't her. It was another woman. Another woman around the age of my mother. She said their healer had been called away to rescue a child in Massawachusett. That she often helped this healer."

"Rabbit Woman."

"Yes. That was her name. She helped me a lot. She was a very good listener. I got the feeling she had lived through a bad... A bad time. Did she?"

"If I am speaking to you as a healer, I have no right to tell you anything of her story. But if I am speaking to you as a storyteller, and if what happened to her will benefit you in any way, then I may tell you.

Were you ever attacked? I mean by a man in that way?"

Flower Stalk shook her head. "Those men don't like me either."

"It's not that they don't like you. They don't want to mate with you."

She laughed and this made her fall back onto the cedars again because she had to move her hands to cover her mouth. "You make them sounds like apli'gmujg, like rabbits."

"Am I that far off?"

Flower Stalk rolled over onto her stomach to bury her laugh in her bearskin blankets.

"If you get right into an acorn, you learn that the only purpose of an oak tree is to make another one of itself. I think that's true of everything."

"So you think that's why some men and women don't like us two-spirited people? Because they can't reproduce with us?"

"What do you think?"

"You healers are all the same. Never saying anything but always asking."

"And…?" This time, I was the one who rolled over to prop my head up using my elbow. I wanted to learn more.

"When I am among men, I feel a certain energy coming toward me. At first. It's not so much toward me as me, but toward me because they think I'm a woman. At first. Do you know what I mean? You're probably right about them being like rabbits. They are always so full of hope, it emanates from them." She smiled. "I feel it emanating from women toward men, too. I am attracted to men. So if I have that energy coming from me toward them, do you think that's what makes them fear me?"

I hadn't thought about that before, but it made sense, and I told her so.

"No wonder I scare them." She was back up on her elbow, too. "I feel better now. Thank you."

"What happened to your friend? Your two-spirited friend. The son of the Chief's sister?"

Flower Stalk rolled over onto her back again, then turned away from me. "I don't want to talk about that."

I said nothing. I waited.

A cloud must have passed over Moon's face because a shadow flickered across the side of the wikuom Flower Stalk was now facing. "He was only seventeen winters old. His mother told him he was better off dead. I know it wasn't her. Not really. I think it was the Fathers who convinced her that her only son was doomed forever and would go to Hell where he would suffer for all eternity if he didn't change his ways." Flower Stalk rolled back again and swept one hand across her private area. "As if this is a choice."

I said nothing.

She looked over at me and I'd never seen such eyes, eyes that were filled with sadness and rage and understanding and hatred all at the same time.

"He killed himself?"

"That he did."

I reached out to caress her shoulder.

"Right in front of me."

Ten

It was morning. We had not been attacked by the Maudits anglaises during the night. I had slept well. Most of us had slept well according to what I heard from the others while we handed out break-fast tea to each other, but I think Flower Stalk had had a restless night. Her face looked even more tired than it had the day before.

"The others will be here soon," she told me as she passed a birch bark cup to Dit Ça who nodded a smile of thanks at her.

Behind her, Bear was shaking out bearskin blankets and putting them back inside the wikuoms.

I filled a birchbark cup and handed it to Francine. "For you, Francine." I was hoping to open a door into her troubled mind. "Did you sleep well?"

"I think so."

"Is that good or bad?" I asked, smiling, trying to keep our conversation light to start with.

"Probably bad. I had the nightmare again."

"Oh?" She was opening up to me already. That was a good sign.

"Wait. Not *probably* bad, definitely bad. I know my family was unharmed in that attack and I know they're coming back to me. But when I have the nightmare, I see them dead." Her seriousness disappeared into a wide-eyed, wide-mouthed and forced smile. "Isn't that the silliest thing you ever heard of?"

"I've heard some very silly things. Do you want to talk about it?"

"Maybe. Sounds like it helped Flower Stalk a little bit last night when she talked about things that bother her. You two went on and on, didn't you?" She went serious again. "Maybe it will help the nightmare go away. What do you think?"

"We could always try, couldn't we? It always helps to talk ab—"

Behind me, Pierre's voice called out much too loudly for the time of day when we should all have been as quiet as possible. "Arrêt. Stop where you are!"

I heard the murmur of several voices, both men and women. Familiar voices.

Then Pierre again, "Oh, it's you."

"So? You have a problem with that?"

No. Please no.

I spun around so fast, I stumbled on the rocks and seashells underneath my moccasins. If Flower Stalk had not been there to catch me, I would have fallen.

It was Second Son! And behind him was Agada, the young girl with the pale-yellow hair and eyes the color of clear blue creek water. There were two men with him, and one other woman, but it was not Solange, Agada's friend with the fox-red hair and piercing green eyes. It was not Solange, that young girl of fifteen or sixteen winters. Solange, who had convinced my husband, Falcon, to go away with her. Most of them held folded travoises.

Second Son spoke before I had the first word out of my mouth.

"Hey, look who's here. It's the great healer. The mighty Keskoua. The magic woman who can save all lives."

I could feel Francine's questioning eyes on me. I didn't need to look at Agada to know she was sending arrows.

Second Son reached into the bag he was carrying and pulled out a bottle of what looked like whiskey. This, he held out toward Pierre. "You look like you could use a shot of this, Pierre Poitou, hein? I know you like it."

Pierre's right hand darted into his jacket and he pulled out one of his little bottles. "Could you perhaps top this up for me?"

"I can do better than that." Second Son reached into his bag again and pulled out another bottle of whiskey. "Take your pick. Neither's all that good, but any port in a storm, right, soldier?"

"Where did you get that? Nobody here will tell me anything." He pulled out his second bottle. "I'm sure you'll let me fill this one up too now, seeing as you have a good supply with you?"

"I hope you brought food," Flower Stalk said, angrily grabbing one of the bottles out of Second Son's hand and, with a mighty swing, throwing it against a pile of rocks where it smashed, spraying the air with bits of glass and a bitter stink.

Pierre Poitou gasped. Second Son growled.

"We all need to keep our wits about us," she said. "What have I told you about bringing that foul poison near me and my people?"

Second Son threw his head back and laughed as he tucked the second bottle of whiskey into his bag. "Your people. That's a joke." He held out his hand to indicate Otter. "I see one." Without turning, he said to Pierre, "Looks like you're out of luck, soldier."

To Flower Stalk, Pierre said, "Merde! Why in the name of God did you do that? I need a drink."

I heard laughter coming from inside the guaq. J-B stepped out into the clearing. "You need whiskey like a duck needs an umbrella, Pierre."

Behind J-B, three young boys I knew were fresh from their Spirit Quest, slapped their hands together and laughed. Another two I did not know were with them. They would be from the next village.

"That's a good one, J-B," said one of them, handing a small package to Otter.

"No 's not," said Second Son, a familiar slur of whiskey suddenly in his words. "It's not funny. It's disrespectful."

The young boys from our village behind J-B—men now, I should call them, since they had finished their Spirit Quest—became instantly serious. It seemed that Second Son had not lost his ability to convince the eager-to-please young that he carried some importance.

Otter bounced the package in his hand. To Flower Stalk he said, "Not very much, but I think we can stretch it. We always can."

Bear had finished putting away all the blankets and I had seen him washing his hands in the little pool by the rocks, a much bigger pool by now with the tide coming in faster and faster.

"Look who's here," he said, coming to stand beside me. Beside? No, more between me and Second Son. "We wondered where you went. Not that anyone cared where you went, just that you went."

I bit my lip to stop myself from agreeing.

"But we did care about J-B and what might have happened to him." Keeping his eyes on J-B's, Bear said, "Marguerite Petitpas, his mother, is frantic with worry. Worrying that he might have joined up with the likes of someone like Second Son. How did Second Son ever talk this young man, this young man with high intelligence and a good spirit within him, to follow a… I won't say the word."

Second Son snorted. "This man is almost twenty winters old and his mama still worries about him?"

Bear held up both hands, his palms facing Second Son. "I am not getting into an argument about whose mama loves somebody better." He turned away and headed toward the hidden wikuom where Otter and the two Acadian men were setting out birchbark dishes and cups.

I immediately embraced J-B, whispering, "He's right you know. Marguerite is almost elue'wiet, crazy, wondering what happened to you. You must find a way to let her know everything is na to´q. But I would not let her know you are spending time with Second Son." With my hands still on his shoulders, I stepped back. "Promise me?"

"I'll explain later."

"It had better be good." I ruffled his hair and pretended to search the guaq behind him and be obvious about it, too. "I see you're alone. Still not married?"

"I'm working on it." Smiling, and waving back at me, he followed the others into the guaq where the bodies lay.

"So I've heard," I called after him before turning toward Agada who was still standing beside Second Son.

She shuffled closer to him. "What do you want?" She hissed at me like a cornered tqoqwej, a wild cat.

With his growling and snorting, and with her hissing, perhaps she and Second Son made a good pair after all: animals to be respected. But animals to keep an eye on at all times if they were near you.

"Where is Solange? Your redheaded friend?"

Agada smiled as though she owned a mirror and had been practicing to look like Second Son when she did it. "I don't think you give a damn in hell where my friend Solange is."

I shrugged. She was right, but only in a way.

"She's going to have a baby and she is sick and your husband won't wake up."

I think the rush of air into me and the squeal out at hearing this was loud enough to frighten the curious birds watching us from the guaq because I heard several sets of wing beats, and even the stirring up of the pine needle carpet behind me as some small creature ran away in fright.

"You asked about my friend first so I will answer you first about her. Seeing as you are so interested. Are you interested?"

I nodded, unsure if I still wanted to hear what would be coming out of Agada's mouth.

"Solange has la grande vérole."

I hadn't heard her come up behind me with a dish of food, but I certainly heard Gisèlle cry out, "Oh, non. Oh, non. Oh doux Jésus Christ. Sauvez-nous de cette maladie sale et dégoûtante. Oh, sweet Jesus Christ. Save us from this dirty, disgusting disease."

I took the dish of food from Gisèlle's shaking hand before she could drop it. "What is this grand whatever you said it was?"

"I have your attention now, don't I, Keskoua?" Agada took one step around behind Second Son's shoulder from where she peeked like a shy child. "It's the great pox."

I said nothing. I knew nothing of this... whatever this was. Gisèlle had used the word "maladie," sickness.

"So the great healer doesn't know everything." Second Son had reached around behind him to move Agada ahead. Now *he* stood like a two-winters-old child behind his mama.

I turned to Gisèlle. "What is this sickness you speak of?"

Dit Ça had moved in beside her and now had one hand on her shoulder in a comforting way. "She is speaking of syphilis. It is widespread among those who dally among those who should not be dallied among."

"Always the joker," said Second Son. He leaned down to whisper into Agada's ear. "What does dally mean?"

From the corner of her mouth, she replied, "How should I know?"

With a partridge leg in her fingers, Flower Stalk pointed to the guaq. "Shouldn't you two be helping your friends there?" To Otter, she said, "This is very good. You'll have to find out how they worked the miracle of making a partridge taste this good using nothing but the partridge."

"Another joker," said Second Son.

"Well? Off you go. You can't be so selfish as to make your friends do all your work. Or perhaps you can."

Putting his arm across Agada's shoulder, he began to lead her toward the guaq.

"Wait," I called out after Second Son. "I want to talk to Agada. Alone."

Flower Stalk shrugged and walked away toward the wikuoms where

Pierre was applying new seaweed and driftwood.

***

"Where's Falcon?" I demanded, as soon as we were out of hearing distance from everyone. "And what do you mean, he won't wake up?"

I hadn't realized how short Agada was and that I was leaning over her like I was a chenoo about to bite off her head and eat it.

I took her by the arm—yes, gently—and led her toward a large piece of driftwood near the shore. The way it lay made it impossible for us to be seen from the water, so we would be safe from both the nosy ears of our group and the dangerous eyes of the enemy.

"Come, let's sit. Even though I would like to be a chenoo right now so I could bite your head off—and I've already thought about doing it, believe me—I won't turn into one until after you've told me everything. Na to´q?"

Her big eyes told me she believed I had a lot more powers than I did.

I sat and patted the driftwood beside me. "You know I'm a joker, too, don't you?"

"Um."

"Sit. I'm a healer, not a hurter."

Her fingers twined in and among each other. She remained standing. "That's not what Second Son said about you. He said you killed his wife."

"I know. He always says that."

"You don't even care?"

"Agada. Sit beside me and tell me about my husband. Please. And no, I don't care. Everyone knows it's not true. Now. Please. Is this what happens to someone with that 'grande vérole' or whatever you call it? Did he catch it from Solange? Do they go to sleep and can't wake up?"

She shook her head. "I don't think so. Nobody said that about it. It's just pox. Sores on the body. And you feel tired and sick and you hurt."

I made more room on the driftwood seat and patted it again. This time she sat.

"It was low tide. I don't really understand how the tides work, just that they're dangerous both coming and going and that after low tide, high tide starts to come in. Falcon and Second Son had come across a foundered ship with a hold full of whiskey, wine and other... What did Flower Stalk call it? 'Foul poison.' Yes. And other foul poison. It's not far from here but well hidden, and they are the only ones who know where it is. Except me. And Solange, too, of course. He actually found two. And he made me promise not to tell Falcon, or Solange, or especially anyone, where that second one is."

Agada watched her fingers intertwine with each other again.

"In one way it was good they had a supply of foul poison because then they didn't get angry with us because there was none. But when there is some..."

I reached out to coil her long, pale hair around the ear on my side so I could see her face, and to let her see my face if she chose to look at me instead of her hands. "You think I've never seen those men at their worst?"

"Solange's sores were really bad. They wouldn't go away no matter what she did. The healer, the one at the village we stay at. She's dead now. She tried to help Solange. She followed us. Followed her. That one day and one day only. She followed Solange. And she was killed! Right there in front of us. Me, Solange and the healer were there on the beach. This beach." She pointed beyond the rocks to an open space. "Right there. We were paying so much attention to what the healer was saying about the illness, about how it might hurt the baby, and about how any healing teas might hurt the baby, that we didn't see the small boat out on the water. We thought they were all gone. I heard they were gone. I can't see very good so I have to let people tell me stuff most of the time. They said the leader of the Rangers was gone and so were they. I think he went but left them behind to do his..." She glanced at me. "Sorry. Then I heard the crack of the—I don't know what it was. Some kind of weapon. Then the healer's head sprayed all over Solange."

My hand automatically went to Agada's back to caress it, to try to ease some of the memory, even though I knew a memory like that never goes away.

"Solange screamed, 'It's my fault. It's all my fault. God is punishing me and everybody around me for being bad. Our stepfather was right about me. I was born evil and I will always be evil. I will always tempt men to their death. And women now, too, it seems.' And then she ran away toward the rocks over there. See those higher ones?"

My eyes followed where her finger was pointing from the end of her outstretched arm.

"The water was coming through really fast. But the rocks were still showing on the bottom of the bay. I think she knew if she jumped off from there, she would at least knock herself out."

"And be drowned."

"Yes. And not be afraid while it was happening."

"But?"

"I cried out for Second Son and Falcon. And even though they were very drunk, they knew what to do and ran to her." As though reliving what had happened, Agada stared at that section of the shore. "I heard more cracks. And once, I saw Falcon slap at his ear. He wasn't hit. We found that out later. But I think it frightened Solange so much, she stopped what she was about to do and turned to look at him.

"He called out to her, and I heard him say, 'No, no. Don't even think of doing it.'"

"Did she? Did she jump?" I knew Falcon all too well. I knew, if she jumped, he would be in the water after her as fast as a chickadee after a seed for its chick.

"I think she changed her mind. She turned toward him and reached out with one arm. But this made her lose her balance. I even saw the small stone she stepped on bounce down from where her foot was. She fell in."

By now, I was able to follow the actions in my own head. I could see Solange's ankle twisting, and the small stone tumble down into the sea. I could see her arms swaying above her as though she were a masgwi, a white birch, in a strong wind. I could see the bulge of the baby in her belly. I could see her topple in. And I could see Falcon jump in after her.

"Second Son went right in after them," said Agada. "He went for Solange first because, he told me after, he knew that Falcon was a strong swimmer."

"That's true. He is. He's good at everything he does."

"He got Solange onto the shore and hidden behind some rocks then went back in for Falcon. Falcon's leg got wrapped around a piece of driftwood and seaweed. Second Son waved for me to come help him."

She looked at me with sad eyes, sad eyes so pale blue they were almost lost in the whites, sad eyes so strange to me, I couldn't look into them anymore. I turned away.

"And I did help," she said. "I truly did. I did the best I could. But people were shooting at us from their boats. I was afraid." She bowed her head to play with her fingers again.

My feelings went out to this young girl. "Now don't you go blaming yourself for something out of your control."

"That's what Flower Stalk told me, too."

"Where is Falcon now? Is he at the other village?"

"Village? There is no village. They are saying there's no longer a village anywhere. They burned everything down. Down flat. Trees, houses, churches, barns, the wheat fields." She swept her arm fully from left to right. "Everything is gone. They even…" She shook her head. "I don't know if I can say it. They burned everything. Everything. Even the cows and the chickens and the sheep." Those strange eyes once again bore into mine. "You could hear them crying out. I never knew a cow could scream." She turned away from me. "I never want to hear that again."

Even though it's always good to let someone talk out something as bad as what Agada had seen and heard, my big worry right then was what was wrong with Falcon. My husband. "If you want to talk about this more, we can do it later. Right now, I need to know where—"

Behind us, J-B's voice spoke, "Ah, there you are, Keskoua. Maman was right. You were always good at playing cache-cache. Especially when there's work to be done."

"That's not true."

"I know. Come help us with the travoises, Agada."

Agada turned to me. "What is this cache-cache?"

J-B answered before I could. "Hide-and-Seek. Did you ever play it where you're from?" To me he said, with a quick tilt of his head toward Agada, "We've decided to make concessions for her today. You-know-who is in a foul mood."

"This is something new about him?"

"We try not to overburden her at any time." To Agada he said, "… because you have to deal with Second Son on a… daily basis. Agada? Ça va bien? Is everything well?"

"We were just talking about Solange. And what happened to Falcon." I rose to my feet. "Where is he?"

"If you want to help us with one of the travoises," answered J-B. "I'll take you to him. But you will have to return on your own if you decide to do so before we return as a group again." He smiled at me. "Although, I'm sure Bear won't let you do that. He'll come up with something he forgot to talk to Flower Stalk about."

"Stop that."

Ignoring Agada's questioning frown, he asked her, "You sure you will be all right?"

Agada rose from the driftwood. "Yes. My travois is loaded?"

J-B nodded, a look of concern for Agada still on his face. "You sure everything is good with you? Did he hit you again? How is your rib from last time?"

One of Agada's hands briefly brushed over her left side. "Has he gone on ahead?"

"What do you think?"

My eyes met J-B's, which were full of compassion for Agada. Then his face turned away as he told Agada, "He wanted to stay close behind Bear. You know. Bear isn't familiar with this area."

"Yes, he is," I said. "He's as familiar with this area as—"

J-B turned to me and his face told me to say no more.

"Ah."

"Your travois is ready, Agada. We gave him a heavy one. Yours weighs not much more than the travois itself, sad to say. You will probably be able to catch up with him. With them." He looked again at me. "Keskoua and I will follow soon. If someone comes back to look for us, would you come with them, please? And make lots of noise?"

I don't think J-B noticed Agada's eyebrows snap closer to each other, it was that quick. Then she looked at her fingers and walked away.

***

"I'm guessing you have something to tell me," I said as I followed J-B to a travois with a small form on it.

"I do. That one's yours."

He lifted one end of the travois for me and helped settle the poles into my hands comfortably.

"It doesn't weigh much. I recommend you don't try to guess what's rolled up inside the blanket on it. Agada's hauling a..." J-B quickly stepped away to a travois with a large form on it. "No. Let's pretend we're all hauling firewood."

"I've never known any firewood that smells like this, but I think you're right. It's best to pretend." I re-adjusted my hands around the poles of my travois and took a few steps forward. J-B was right. The bundle on my travois weighed so little, I dared not try to guess the age of the child wrapped in the filthy blanket on it. "So, are you going to tell me your big secret now? Or am I going to have to torture it out of you?"

"Hush." J-B touched a finger to his lips, to one ear, then to the guaq behind us.

From out of the trees came one of the young Spirit Questers I had only just met. "Just relieving myself," he said, patting the front of his clothing. "I can take that for you, Keskoua. There is no need for you to come with us. You can stay behind with the powerful Chief and help her. E´e? Like Pierre is doing?" He was making his eyes narrow so I wouldn't be able to read what was behind them.

"No," said J-B, much more harshly than I'd ever heard him speak before. "You will run on ahead, as fast as you can, catch up with the others and offer your services to any of them who need it. Keskoua and I wish to discuss the health of my mother and this is none of your business nor anyone else's. Run along now."

The young Spirit Quester hesitated. His eyebrows stayed together longer than Agada's had but they soon smoothed out. "Na to´q. But it's just that Second Son told me to make sure you would be all right. That I should help you. That I—"

"Thank you, but it's not my first time in the bush, is it? Nor Keskoua's first time in the bush, either. Run along."

I could tell by the boy's hesitating movements that he didn't want to go against what Second Son had ordered him to do, but when J-B stretched himself up to his full height and pushed out his chest, the boy turned and ran.

"What will Second Son do to him?" I asked.

J-B shrugged. "Nothing he hasn't done before. Now." His voice went quiet. "We must listen to make sure no one else is around to hear us before I begin to tell you of the dangers that face your beloved."

"Falcon?"

"No, silly. Bear."

Eleven

"I think it's safe for us to talk now," J-B said. "But let's not use any names. Directly."

"What is all this intrigue?"

"Listen to her. 'Intrigue.' New word?"

"Yes, a new word. Marguerite gets books not only from the Settlement at Quebec, but from France, too. And when a shipment of wool comes for her from New England—when they ever do, these days—there are always books for her from there as well."

J-B laughed.

"What's funny?"

"You think you're telling me something new?"

"Ah. Does Marguerite force you to read all these books she buys?"

"Not only that, she forces me to write reports on them. Not the English ones, though. I still can't make much sense of those at all no matter how hard I try. She insists on testing me with the French ones, though. To ensure that I've read them from beginning to end. Like Geneviève made you do."

Now I laughed.

"Try living in a community when all your friends know that your mother makes you read love stories." I heard him grunt.

"Bad enough having your mother tell you what to read. But giving you tests on it?" I set my travois down on the ground. "I must not disrespect the remains of this young person by laughing too much." With a wave of my hand I indicated the small body under the dirty blanket on the travois. I opened and closed my hands several times before picking up the poles of my travois again. "Is it true? What Flower Stalk said? That all of her people were killed?"

J-B set his travois down and stretched his hands like I had done. "Yes and no." He tipped one hand back and forth making it look like a raft on a lake on a windy day. "Mostly no." He picked up his travois again. "Many were killed, yes. You saw that yourself. You have one on your travois." He pointed. "The blanket is slipping off."

I adjusted the blanket.

"I think it was just too overwhelming for her—you know that word?"

I did.

"Looks like we read the same books."

"I'm guessing some of them escaped but she doesn't know who."

"Some of them are staying at the village we're going to. They're too terrified to come out of hiding."

I was grateful we had come to a path. Pulling my travois over rocks and between trees was not easy.

"No, no, Keskoua. Not on the path. Never on the path." His voice became a whisper. "We've already come too close." He indicated a rocky opening between two large kaksk'ug, cedars.

As we passed through them, I whispered to J-B, "Do we have time? My munti is low on kaksk´us. I should harvest some."

"Time, we have, but we're too close to the path to be safe. You'll have to wait."

I was not surprised to hear that Flower Stalk had misled me into thinking that all her people were gone. They were all gone, that part was true. But she didn't know who was gone from being dead and who was gone from being somewhere else.

"Your special love is in great danger," said J-B.

"I know, that's why I am going with you. To see why he won't wake up."

J-B actually said, "Hee hee."

"What?"

"I mean your other special love."

I stopped walking and if my hands had not been on the travois, they would have been on my hips. "Would you please stop saying that about us. I mean about him. I mean about me."

J-B had propped one leg under a handle of his travois and was covering his mouth with that hand to silence himself. His eyes shone with laughter.

"Just stop. Na to´q? Stop."

J-B got himself under control and took hold of the travois's handle once again. "You said us."

I closed my eyes and shook my head.

"I'm sorry, Keskoua. I didn't mean to laugh. Things are very serious for your... 'friend.' His life is in danger." J-B slowed his pace to get his travois through an area with loose rocks and stones. He propped his travois against a boulder, then came back to help me.

"How is his life in danger any more than any of the rest of us here?"

J-B's eyes met mine directly. "Someone is envious of his position in the village back home. Do you know what I'm saying?"

I did.

"Someone still thinks he is hereditary Chief. And when I listen to him when it's his turn with the Talking Stick, when he speaks to those young boys, I fear not only for the life of your 'friend,' but for the lives of many others in your village. The lives of those who support your 'friend.'"

"I'm glad you told me about this, J-B. What can we do about it?"

J-B did not reply, and I had too many thoughts in my own head to form even one of them into a suggestion, so I kept quiet, too, as we continued to make our way through the rough terrain.

At certain spots along our way, it took great effort to get our travoises over, through and around the piles of rocks and trees, but we made progress.

***

My stomach was beginning to rumble just as I got to the top of what J-B had told me was the final rise. I put my hands over it, hoping to soothe it. I was out of breath from climbing and dragging a travois behind me, so J-B had brought mine up for me and had gone down the hill again to bring his up.

I was watching him, so did not hear or see the woman who came up behind me. I jumped when she spoke.

"Show me your hands," she spat.

I turned toward her.

She looked like our people but I knew she was Acadian, too. She was around fifty winters old. Her narrowed eyes went from my face to my stomach and back again several times. "What are you hiding there?"

For the first time, I noticed the pistol she was waving, also from my face to my stomach.

"In your hands? Answer me, putain." The pistol darted upwards like a so´qomu´jl, a minnow, reaching for a bug on the water above him.

Putain? This woman was calling me a whore? "Excuse me. What did you say? And watch where you're pointing that thing."

Just then, J-B came into view part way down the hill. "Merde, this is getting heavier every step I take." He glanced upwards. "Oh, bonjour, madame. I see you've met Keskoua. She is from our village. She is our healer." At first, I thought J-B's grunt of effort this time was faked, but looking back on it, I know he grunted because he made a mistake in letting this woman know I was a healer.

The pistol in the woman's hand disappeared behind her back. I don't know where she tucked it, but when her short fingers came out toward me to shake hands, it was gone.

"Ah, welcome, fellow healer." Her lips smiled but her eyes did not.

From below, "Help me with this, would you, Keskoua?"

I could see nothing that J-B needed help with, but I scampered down to him anyway.

"Grab the other handle and help me over this rock," he instructed.

This put our heads close together.

Without moving his lips, J-B whispered to me, "She is no healer."

We did our best to make it look like getting J-B's travois over this tiny rock was the most difficult thing we had ever done.

"She does seem rather... What's that word? Ah... unpleasant. And you say she is a liar, too?"

Aloud, J-B demanded, "Can you not do better than that?"

"I guess I am too weak and stupid to know how to do it right. Right?"

J-B turned his face away from me toward the bottom of the hill. Again whispering, he said, "Cut it out, will you? Don't make me laugh. Especially in front of her."

Working together, we got the travois up to the top of the hill, but not before J-B managed to warn me more against this woman. "She can be nasty. Careful. Go along with everything she says."

The woman threw her arms around J-B and kissed both his cheeks. "I'm so happy you made it back safely. You are such a wonderful young man to come help us like this. All the way from your village."

"Well actually," I said. "He doesn't exactly live in our village."

Quickly, J-B escaped this woman's grasp and reached toward me.

"And besides, he came here to—"

He slapped his hand on my shoulder as if to demonstrate me to a visiting slave trader, then squeezed hard enough to stop me in midsentence.

"This is Keskoua, our storyteller. Keskoua, this is Matuwes. She is very important in her village. Aren't you, Matuwes?"

I didn't know her well enough yet to know whether the name, Matuwes, Porcupine, suited her or not, but I would try my best never to get too close—in any way—to this new acquaintance.

Twelve

W e followed Matuwes the remaining short distance to her village. I assumed that J-B had been through here many times, but he was acting like he hadn't ever been. I guessed this was so he could let her describe everything, either to prove something to me, or because he wouldn't have been able to get a word in anyway.

And describe she did. Every time we passed a plant growing alongside the trail we were taking, she would describe its use. But out of perhaps twelve plants, she would have poisoned eight people. J-B was right. She was no healer.

When we arrived at the makeshift village, I counted eighteen wikuoms in the clearing, and in the trees behind them, three small ones. I knew that the ones in the trees would most likely be used by women during their Moon Time. Moon Time wikuoms were usually farther away from the village, so having them this close, told me that something had superseded tradition here, too. The puffs of smoke with small bits of what looked like black feathers, but what I knew were not, rising in the air above the trees beyond the Moon Time wikuoms, told me where the Acadian village had been. A man with hands and forearms wrapped in cloth was working with two young boys at setting up another wikuom between two freshly chopped-down trees. I would say the boys were our people and the man most likely Acadian by the clothes he was wearing, even though these had burnt patches and were barely anything I could call clothes at all. With them was a tall, muscular woman with thick braids and dark skin. She seemed familiar to me but her back faced me so I could not say for certain that I knew her.

We were approached by a tall, handsome man about forty winters old. His hair was not braided, but twisted into long, thick strands that went all the way down past his shoulders. He was dressed like our people, but I knew he was not one of us. His skin was dark and his nostrils wide. There was something familiar about him, too, and it made Captain KrommeZee and his ship, the *Rita Petronella*, jump into my head. I told myself to ask this man later if he had come here from the harbor in Boston with Captain KrommeZee. And I would ask him if I seemed familiar to him.

With this man was a young girl of perhaps ten winters. She, too, had dark skin and was dressed as our people dress. This girl threw her arms around J-B's waist and hugged him tight.

"You are safe once again," she said in our language.

"That I am. Thanks to my friend Keskoua, here, I am safe from evil chipmunks and poisonous robins."

The girl laughed and grabbed J-B's hand. "Come with me. Celeste has to help with the dikes today, so I get to show you where they hid the food and water this time. You must be starved."

The tall, handsome man stepped toward me with his hand extended. "I am Makena. They call me Mak. And you are? My niece's friend J-B called you… What? Kes…?"

"Keskoua. It means—"

J-B called back over his shoulder, "It means Pain In The Arse. At least, that's what my father says."

The young girl with J-B hid her smile behind her free hand.

"And he says she lives up to the name."

The tall, handsome man called Mak turned to Matuwes. "Get her some tea. Can't you see she's exhausted?"

"Yes, Mak. Right away. I'll get that right away. Do you wish for some, too?" She looked up at him with big round eyes like a baby lentug's, a baby deer's.

When her eyes turned in my direction, I saw the soul of a chenoo in behind them. When she passed me, she whispered, "Hah. Exhausted? I am the one exhausted. Running here, running there. No rest."

I turned to Mak. "Who is Chief here?"

"That would be me now. Imagine that. The head person of a village in his own land far across the sea, captured by a neighboring tribe, sold to slave traders, shipped across the ocean to an island, taken away from that island by ship to end up being shot on the docks at Boston Harbor, put onto another ship—the *Rita Petronella*, her captain ended up naming her—delivered to Port Royal, from where he managed to get here…" Mak spread his hands wide. "… along with his sister and her newborn child, to become, through terrible circumstances, ten winters later, the head person in *this* village."

"Curly?" I said. "Is it really you? No. Not Curly. Makena. Yes. Your name is Makena. Now I remember. After all this time? Let me look at you." I walked around him. "You look a lot better than the last time I saw you. You were bones with skin hanging off them."

"Let me look at you, too. I can't remember much. The medicines you gave me were strong. You were dressed as a Puritan. Your hair is different. Much different."

"You did nothing but sleep."

"Except for the changes in your fashion, you haven't changed at all over these ten years." He raised my chin with gentle fingers. "Ah, I mean ten winters. I'm still trying to get my head around that expression." He smiled. "I was somewhat awake when I slept so I should have recognized you instantly today. My apologies. And I can't remember if I ever thanked you. If I didn't then, I thank you now."

I took a step back. "I'm surprised you remember anything at all. I'm surprised you even survived. Do you remember when they put you into that huge traveling case? To get you from the inn to the ship?"

"With a newborn baby, no less. Oh, I remember it well. Too well. How could I forget something like that?"

The baby. The young girl with J-B would be that baby. "Yes, of course. I'd almost forgotten about the baby. I can't imagine what that would have been like."

"No. You couldn't. And I would not want you to even try." He turned his face away from me. "But I've experienced worse."

I'd heard about conditions in the holds of slave ships. Mak was right. I could not imagine what it would be like to lie in one position, body to body, for weeks—even months—on end with very little exercise and unfamiliar food.

It was my turn to reach out to him. We embraced and held each other for a long time.

"You disappeared soon after we arrived in Port Royal."

"Afia—my sister—" He pointed to where the man in the bandages was working. "That's her. Over there."

"I thought I recognized her from somewhere. She looks a lot better, too, than the last time I saw her."

Afia, as though she had felt us looking at her and talking about her, turned to raise her hand and send us a smile.

"She wanted to be as far away from a port as possible. She was determined never to be put on another ship. Besides that, Captain KrommeZee thinks it best to have us—what does he call us? Ah, yes. The Newly Arrived." He smiled. "Willem thinks it best we scatter."

My frown made him continue.

"Look at me," he said. "We can easily hide in a forest at night, but with our dark skin, we stand out in a crowd of light-skinned people."

"And?"

"If we become the crowd...?"

Ah. I understood. "You are being transported here secretly, so you can't draw attention to yourselves."

"Singly, we will no doubt go unnoticed. Those who would be concerned would assume we are still slaves and would be content with that."

I hadn't realized we'd been moving along together toward the same area of the clearing that J-B and the young girl had gone to. They had already passed through the line of, perhaps, twenty people who waited to receive meals of meat, berries, and tea or water. The young girl had followed J-B to an empty space on one of the logs people were sitting on. There was room for J-B to sit but he had remained standing.

"How do you prepare this much food without drawing attention to the cooking fires? Flower Stalk can get away with it because there are so few people there."

J-B overheard me. "Look around you, Keskoua."

I did.

"I mean, look up. Past the trees. What do you see?"

"Smoke. Everywhere."

"We have fires only where it's thickest."

"Very smart. Whose idea was that?"

J-B's hands held a dish of food and a birch bark cup, so he pointed with his elbow. "The man behind you." He set his cup down behind the log and picked a piece of something thin and brown out of his dish. "It's amazing what happens when people from different parts of the world get together and share their knowledge. Isn't it?"

Mak spread his hands, palms up, and shrugged. "It's not just me."

"That's why they chose my uncle over everybody else to take over when they... when Lnu Saqamaw... when he... when Chief Api..." The young girl looked down at her dish of food. "You know. When Chief Apistanewj got burned."

"What is your name, little one?" I set my munti down beside her.

Her eyes sought those of her uncle.

"Go ahead," he said. "There's nothing to be ashamed of."

Mak handed me a dish of food before taking one for himself from an Acadian man standing beside the empty fire pit.

Mak shrugged again. "Sorry for the meagreness of your dish. Even though it would probably be safe to have a fire here to cook our food, we do not want to risk it unless we have to. This meat came to us cooked." He turned to point beyond the Moon Time wikuoms. "Over there, behind those trees, where the Acadian village—everyone's village, I suppose—used to be, there's an unburned shed where we take turns boiling water for tea. The roof is broken, so the smoke from that small fire gets spread out and goes unnoticed. At least we can have tea whenever we want." He indicated my cup and said, "I wish we could serve it hotter, but the shed is in an open space. You understand that makes it very dangerous for those who go to and from there. By the time they go from behind tree to behind tree—whatever trees are still standing, that is—the water is cold again."

"And that's why everyone takes turns? Whose idea was that?"

"It was a general consensus."

"A general what?"

"Consensus. It means agreement."

"Alors, Keskoua! Another new word for you!"

"*My* tea is hot enough," said the young girl. "And I'm not ashamed having no name. All I have to do is remain patient. Do you know what that word means?"

"Oh, she knows the meaning." J-B popped a berry into his mouth. "It's just that she's never experienced it." Into his mouth went another berry.

The young girl looked up at me with great seriousness. "Is that true?" She glanced behind her at the grinning J-B, back to me, then back to J-B.

"I guess it must be true." Then balancing her dish of food on her knees, she began to sort through it. "I mean, I don't have an *official* name yet. Mama and Uncle call me Little Gracie. After the nice lady—Mama says she was really nice—who helped me be born."

"I met her," I said. "And yes, she is very nice. Did you know I was there right after you were born?"

"Were you really?" She glanced back at J-B again for confirmation.

"Yes, I was."

A frown passed over her face.

"What's wrong?"

"I'm glad they didn't decide to call me by *your* name, then."

Everyone within hearing distance laughed. Everyone but Little Gracie. And me.

"The Grandmothers and Grandfathers are still trying to think of a name for me. But they're taking a long time. One of the Grandmothers— she got... she got killed by... by *them*. She told me if I didn't remain patient, they would give me the name Impatience."

The woman at the far end of the log said, "I was there when she said that, chérie. She was only teasing you."

"She said I wouldn't want that name." Little Gracie picked out a gmu´jminn, a raspberry, and placed it daintily into her mouth. "She said that would make me sound like a goddamned Puritan."

Trying to hide my laugh, I quickly glanced up at Mak who opened his eyes wide and lifted his eyebrows along with his shoulders.

I couldn't begin to count how many times I had gotten away with something when I was a child. It seemed that things never changed.

I sorted through my own dish to pick out several berries. I had always thought berries were berries, but somehow, these gmu´jming were better than any I had ever tasted. But I poked at a piece of the meat in my dish with my finger. It felt much firmer than I was used to. "What is this meat?

Or is it meat? It has a texture unfamiliar to me."

"Beef is not very good when it's overcooked," Mak answered. "But we have little choice. Even if the deer and moose had not run off, we can't be firing shots that can be heard by them. We had someone cut down two cedars to make arrows from, but we have only one bow."

"Beef?"

"Cow," Little Gracie told me, now working hard at chewing what was obviously a piece of it in her mouth. "They burned them all. Uncle told me. So we decided to take advantage."

J-B pulled a strip of heavily chewed—so flattened—cow meat out of his mouth and set it on one side of his dish. "If it's cooked properly, it's quite good. Please realize that Benny has burned almost everything in the area so there is no food whatsoever. Like Mak said, we might soon have arrows, but there are very few of the good trees left for making bows to shoot them from. If and when the larger animals return." He took several gulps of tea from his birch bark cup and set it back down behind the log. "If you think this is bad, this dried out cow meat…" With finger and thumb, he picked up his piece of chewed meat and flipped it around. "… I don't even think a fish would go for this if you put it on a hook. Like I said, if you think beef is bad, you should try a chicken that's been through a fire."

"Surely there must be something other than this." I picked up the small piece of meat on my plate and bit into it. My mother was admired in our village for the high quality of her pemmican, but I was never one of the admirers. Pemmican had never been one of the things I liked to eat. This "cow" would be another. Many times, I had helped the Mother of One-Eyed Joe prepare a hide. Chewing on this cow was even worse than chewing on a bull moose hide that had been salted and soaked in its own brains and left out to dry for days. Much worse.

"I'm very sorry, Keskoua," Mak said, and the look on his face told me he meant it. "But you yourself know we need to consume meat. For our health. And this is all that's available. And even though it has been cooked beyond cooking, it might still go bad in a matter of days and then we will have nothing. It is best you try to consume some of it. Try to chew as much juice out of it as you can."

Mak was right. We needed to eat meat, especially the young ones. I didn't think there would have been time to grow beans in this new area. I would ask where they had grown their food supplies in the old village. Yes, I would ask, even though I knew what the answer would probably be.

"It's not so bad when you get used to it." Little Gracie said this in a way I knew she had heard from the Grandmothers and Grandfathers as a strict command and didn't really believe it herself. "Really. It's not that bad." Like J-B had done, she pulled a string of chewed, dried up meat out of her mouth and set it on the edge of her dish. "If I get two or three of those, and dry them out, maybe I could make a nice bracelet out of them. What do you think? Do you think it would work?"

I looked at the piece of dried-up cow between my fingers. I looked at Little Gracie whose face showed more concern for my well-being than I had ever seen on anyone else's face.

"I'm trying to think of something good about eating burnt cow," she said. "To help you, you know, be able to eat it. Uncle says we need it. Please, Keskoua, help me make a bracelet."

I took a deep breath, stuck the piece of dried-out meat into the edge of my mouth, and gnawed on it like it was a piece of pine bark and I had been starving for half a moon. What can I tell you it tasted like? Like nothing I'd ever eaten before, and like nothing I would ever want to eat again.

I sensed her before I saw her, so didn't flicker when Matuwes stuck a cup of tea under my nose.

"Peppermint tea should help get that nasty taste of dried-up beef out of your mouth."

"Why, thank you ever so much, Matuwes. How kind of you to bring me tea when you yourself must be exhausted beyond reason." I didn't dare look at J-B, or anyone else for that matter. I continued. "Please tell me you have brought along a cup of this…" I leaned over to take a deep sniff of the tea she had given me. It smelled like peppermint, so I assumed it would be safe for me to drink. I took a sip. "… delightful peppermint tea. But where is your own? Please, you must rest yourself. Running here, running there. And at your advanced age, too."

I heard someone spit out what was either tea or water, then cough. I think it was J-B. I didn't dare turn to look at him.

"I can understand how reluctant you are to do much of anything other than attempt to remain in the good graces of the handsome Mak."

Matuwes's mouth opened and shut like a mtesgm, a snake, trying to swallow something too big for its head, but before any words came out of it, one of the Spirit Questers came running up to Mak.

He was out of breath. "Seven of them. Seven. Seven men. With muskets. Maybe more. I saw seven but I heard a lot more voices."

Mak took in a deep breath and cried out in the voice of a ga´qaquj, a crow. Four quick caws: *caw caw caw caw*. Then six, a pause, then two. *caw caw caw caw caw caw, caw caw*. He repeated this.

Immediately, everyone around me, taking their dishes and cups and hats, and everything else that was laying near them, scattered into the trees.

Before I could react and grab my munti, it was in the hands of Matuwes who was already halfway across the clearing.

From behind me, a hand reached around to cover my mouth and an arm went around my waist. "Not a sound," whispered Mak. "Not a single sound." He released me. "This way." And he grabbed my wrist and pulled me along with him toward a huge pile of rocks.

"But she's got my munti."

"Right now, your life is more important than your healing bag. Keep quiet and stay apace with me."

I had little choice as this man's hand was twice as big as mine, and the strength and power of it would make it impossible for me to do otherwise.

"And don't drop your dish or cup. If they find anything recently used, they'll know there are people here."

"Do you really think they would kill us?"

"Without a doubt."

Thirteen

I followed Mak toward the overgrown area that J-B and I had recently come through.

"Over here," he said, veering off toward a steeper section of the rise. "There's an old creek bed we can hide in. I've used it before. You'll see. It's quite roomy. Almost comfortable."

I was out of breath by the time we reached the hiding place Mak had been describing, and I'm proud to say I had not dropped my dish or cup. Mak released my wrist.

"Set those down beside mine here and help me move this log."

"You mean this one?" Mak already had his arms around a huge limbless cedar. I reached down at my end, ready to lift.

With one hand, he beckoned me closer. "No, no. You'll break your back. We need to lift at the same section of the tree. I know it doesn't look like it, but this is a fresh-cut log, so extra heavy."

Carefully, making sure I didn't slip on any of the large stones and tree roots between me and Mak, I made my way to the top end of the log that lay against a huge boulder. Once, I lost my balance and put my hand out against the log to steady myself. When I removed my hand, I noticed my palm was covered with soot. "Well done." I looked more closely at the other logs piled over the creek bed. They had all been made to look old. "Who did this? No one would ever know that Mother Earth was not involved."

"Believe it if you will or don't. It was Matuwes."

Ah. My new acquaintance, The Porcupine, was good at hiding things.

"She thought of it and directed us. In no time, it was completed. There are two other hides. Over there and over there." He pointed with his head.

I looked quickly to see one head disappearing downwards and at the other hide, six arms lifting a big tree trunk from one side to above their now-hidden heads then down.

"Hurry. Help me lift this."

I helped him slide the big log over far enough to allow us to squeeze into the space below. I snatched up his dish and mine and both our cups. Once below, Mak stood under the log and lifted it over us.

"There's food and water here. But right now, we must pretend we are dead and buried in this hole. Make no sound."

Fourteen

We had been in the creek bed hideaway for what seemed like half a moon. I think it felt that way because I could hear the rustle of dried leaves and pine needles being stepped on, over and over, but I heard no human voices. Once, the squeal of a frightened and angry apalqaqamej, chipmunk, told me I was not imagining that Mak and I were being hunted like a paqtesmul with the clenched-jaw illness, a wolf with rabies. But now it was quiet. I think that was worse.

Mak was already very close to me and had even wrapped his arms around me, but I hadn't thought about that until an owl hooted close by. I jumped and Mak's arms got tighter.

Moon was almost full but down here in the creek bed, the logs, branches and moss over the hiding place to protect us from being seen, prevented us from seeing much of anything, either.

After a long while of silence, I whispered, "Are they gone?"

"The tide will be out by now. They don't usually leave anybody here alone. If you ask me, that's because they're all such little babies."

"I think most of them are little babies. The soldiers at the fort are. Barely sixteen winters, some of them."

"But Spirit Questers are only… What? Thirteen winters? And then they're men. Men who can be trusted."

"Our boys are better prepared, though. Aren't they? From birth."

"True. Very true. As are our boys from my home village." Mak made no move to loosen his arms around me when he said, "We're probably safe now."

"Only probably?" I wriggled away from him and felt an immediate chill. He had been keeping me warm. "It's cold down here."

"That's why I was holding you. I'm sorry if I made you feel uncomfortable. I just thought... You know." He slid away from me. "I think there's a bearskin in here somewhere. I'll try to find it."

"Did I make you feel uncomfortable, too?" I could neither see him nor hear him, but I could sense his presence. "If I did, I'm sorry."

Then his semi-whisper came from the far corner of the hide. "You're forgiven. Aha. Here it is. And I don't feel anything crawling around on it either." A pause, then more whispering. "Oh wait, what's this? Ow, ow. Oh no. It's eating my arm off. It's going to get you, too. Oh no."

I was able to hold in my laughter. "Stop it. Maybe there's someone still out there and they'll hear us."

"I'm trying my best to be a gentleman and lighten the atmosphere. It's not every day I get to lie down in a secret hideaway with a beautiful woman. Or, perhaps, I should say it's not every *night* I get to lie down in a secret hideaway with a beautiful woman."

"And you can stop that, too. I was just talking to someone else about this very thing. This thing of tension between men and women when they are together, especially alone together. Because of what you have said to me, I am thinking you feel it, too?"

"Oh yes. I think every man faces conflict when he is alone with a woman, not just a beautif—"

"Don't do that."

"Sorry. When a man is alone with a woman—and I'm speaking of myself, of course, it's not exactly a standard topic of conversation when men are together—we tend to... I don't really know how to explain it. I think when a man is alone with a woman, he feels obliged to make a play for her because he assumes she is expecting it from him? That he would not be a man if he did not make a play for her? Does that make any sense?"

I nodded even though I knew he couldn't see me do it.

He covered me with the bearskin and tucked it along my sides like we do when we are saying good night to our children.

"Well? Does it?"

"You would, wouldn't you. You would ask me to continue. To expand." I could hear him lie down next to me.

I turned to face him and pulled the bearskin up under my chin as I did so. "Perhaps I should ask you directly. When I was speaking with this person, I found myself wondering why I was afraid, and afraid isn't the right word but that's the closest I can come to it, why I was afraid to be with men. Alone, as you say. I thought it was only because when I was a young woman, I was forced to do something I did not want to do. So now I am thinking that every man wants to do that to me. In your experience... or... maybe that's not the right word either. Maybe I should say: from what you have seen in your life."

Mak said nothing.

"That was a question, you know."

"I know."

"As far as you know, do all men... What's that word the Fathers use? Ah, yes. Do all men lust after women?"

I felt his fingers caress my forehead. There was no "lust" in them. I felt nothing but concern emanating from his hands or from him.

"I would say so, yes. It's the way we are made." He rolled away from me. "Now for the big question." I couldn't see his face in the dark, but I knew he was smiling when he said this.

I was happy he could not see the smile on my own face. "Please notice that I am no longer asking you to continue."

"No? You don't want to know what I want to know?"

I rolled away from him again. "I think, yes. I think women lust after men, too."

"Are you in agreement, then, that besides the two of us now—and perhaps that friend you were speaking with—we are the only people in the whole world who know that men lust after women and women lust after men?"

"That friend is Flower Stalk. And we were speaking of the fear men must feel being attracted and repelled by her at the exact same time. That it must be confusing enough to bring the rage of denial up like a wall between them and her. The attraction is natural, isn't it? As though we were," and here, I laughed, "rabbits. That's what she said. Rabbits. We are nothing more than two-legged rabbits lusting after other two-legged rabbits."

I heard him shift in the darkness. "I wouldn't go *that* far." I knew he was trying to sound stern, but he wasn't doing a very good job of it.

"And thinking that we might be getting overtaken at any moment and held down on the ground by a two-legged rabbit, turns us into a frightened chipmunk."

This time, Mak laughed. "I am actually picturing the transformation of these creatures and their activities. I'm glad there are only three of us in the world who see things this way or the population would be decimated and reduced to nothing."

"Except for the three of us."

Mak laughed again. "Two of whom would be lusting after me forcing me to choose between you."

"Go to sleep," I said.

"You first."

"I think not."

Fifteen

Once more, I'd had a good sleep. I didn't want to admit it, but I think having an extra pair of ears, Mak's ears, helped. And I think, inside my mind, while I slept, Falcon was there, too, beside me like he had been in the old days before Solange.

Good sleep or not, I was soon back into worrying.

Mak and I had climbed out of the creek bed, we had put the big log back over it, and were making our way back to the area of the temporary village, when, from the bush on Mak's side, came a woman's voice.

"There you are, Keskoua. Wait. I'm doing myself up."

"I'll go on ahead," said Mak. "If things seem amiss, I'll double back and get you. If you don't see me soon, that will mean all is well."

From out of the trees came Agada adjusting her skirt. "Nobody could find you. Where were you two?" She gave me that special smile that only passes between women who think they know each other's secrets. "No, you don't need to answer my question. I know you will give me one answer. That answer will either be a lie or not a lie and I won't know which is which anyway." She untied the belt around her waist, tied it, undid it and tied it again.

"Here. Let me do that." I stepped in, pushed her hands away, undid the knot and retied it for her. "There."

She was no longer touching the knot on her belt, but her fingers were still moving as though they were tying and untying knots.

I put both my hands over hers. "Stop doing that with your fingers. What has you so upset? Something extra is going on, isn't it?" I leaned down and turned my head sideways so I could look up into her face through her hair. I tucked one side of her hair behind an ear. "Agada? What has happened?"

She seemed to come out of a trance. When she let out her breath, I could smell the previous night's whiskey.

"Try to remember."

"Oh, yes. That's right. Solange. The baby. The baby is coming. The baby is finally coming."

Finally? This puzzled me. These young women had come into the lives of Second Son and Falcon only six moons ago. Falcon could not be the father. "The baby is not early?"

Agada shook her head. "No. It is late. Very late. The healer told her the baby was dead inside her."

As usual, my mouth spoke my thoughts. "Falcon is not the father."

Agada laughed. "Not unless his, uh… his *kønsorganer*…" She pointed to her private area. "I think in French it is called organes génitaux? He cannot be the father unless his organes génitaux are magical and can be many miles and many months away from here whenever the desire strikes him."

Sixteen

Relieved to learn that Falcon was not the father of Solange's child, I followed Agada to the temporary village, and was even happier to see a line of people getting food of some kind put into their dishes. From where I was, to me, it looked like cow again. I would ask someone later where they had planted their three sisters. Perhaps something—even a little—had survived the fires of the Maudits anglaises. Even a kernel of corn or a single bean would be better than dried-up cow.

A quick count told me everyone was present. Not everyone was na to´q, though. Some were coughing, and the women holding babies had such thin, strained faces, I knew they were giving every bit of food to their children and eating only enough to keep their milk from drying up.

Mak, J-B and Bear came up to me at exactly the same time from three different directions.

"As you can see, all is well," said Mak.

"Maybe for you," I said, as I saw a young woman with a baby almost crumple to the ground. The older woman with her had prevented that. Then the older woman, even though the young one tried to stop her, took the baby to hold it.

"I found out where Falcon is," said J-B.

"Fine. But where is Matuwes? She has my munti. I need it before I can help anyone."

Bear's mouth said nothing but his eyes did. They said the same thing Agada had said, that there was no point in asking a question because the answer, "no," would either be a lie or not a lie.

"Follow me," said J-B, heading off in the direction I had just come from. "I hope you're up for a wet walk, the tide seeps in close to where they are. Makes a real mess. The Maudits anglaises don't like getting their feet wet, the big babies."

Mak looked over at me and smiled. "See? I'm not the only one who thinks like that."

"So we figured—Mak figured—hiding Falcon in the middle of a seawater swamp might do the trick. The uh... That... The girl is there too."

"Her name is Solange," Agada snapped.

"It's na to´q, J-B. It is not Falcon's baby."

"I know," he called back.

"You know? You knew? You didn't tell me?"

"Yes. The baby. The baby is coming out finally." said Mak.

"Agada told me that. Just now. Very sad but I wish someone had bothered to let *me* know."

Beside me, Agada bobbed her head up and down. Then her glance told me she thought I was accusing her of something.

"It's na to´q," I told her. "It wasn't just you..." and my voice rose here, "... *keeping this important information from me.*"

"Why sad?" Like me, Bear could not have known about Solange's baby. We had just arrived. "The birth of a baby should be a time of celebration. It looks like they don't have much here for a feast, but we could try. Right, Mak? We must try. And what are you talking about, Keskoua? What information? What am I missing out on here?"

"Come on," J-B called out to me. "Hurry. Stop talking and move."

I strode off to follow J-B.

"Or," said Bear, jumping in behind to follow me. "Are you saying the baby will have the same illness as the mother?" He grabbed my arm. He was not going to leave this alone.

Mak put his hand on Bear's arm.

Agada kept walking behind J-B.

"It is not right to hate a baby—or anyone—because of a disease. You know that." Bear let my arm go and turned back toward Mak. "If I were Lnu Saqamaw here, I would not allow anyone to hate anyone. No matter what. There is too much hate in the air already."

Mak made a respectful bow of his head to Bear, "The baby is dead inside her."

Bear whirled to face me again. "Is this true, Keskoua?"

"So I have been told. I will not know until it comes out of Solange." I turned away from him. "J-B, wait for me."

As I sloshed through the thin layer of seawater covering almost everything in this area, I heard Bear's voice.

"Mesgei´. I am sorry, Mak. I did not know."

Mak's answer faded from my hearing as I hurried away. "It is not something everyone is experienced with…"

***

Before long, we had reached what could not ever be called a wikuom, but what was still a shelter of sorts. It was set on a slight rise, almost like an island in the middle of this seawater swamp. More of those imitation logs that had protected the creek bed Mak and I had stayed in, had been stacked up like lean-tos and covered in seaweed and cedar. There were three of these shelters, and the way they faced each other, made them look like they were a continuation of the small hill they'd been built on.

I could hear moaning from inside one of them and the unmistakable voice of Matuwes scolding the moaner. As much as I did not want to be any kind of comfort to the woman who had taken my husband from me, I was a healer. I would never speak to anyone the way The Porcupine was speaking to this girl.

I took a deep breath and slipped between the seaweed-and-moss-covered logs and branches.

Over to one side lay the still, unmoving body of Falcon who appeared to be sleeping peacefully. As much as I wanted to go to him first, a glance over at Matuwes and the girl, Solange, told me I could not. Falcon had to wait. At least his chest was moving up and down.

There lay Solange, legs open in childbirth, and with one leg and one arm of a baby protruding from her. I could tell the baby was a boy.

"What in the name of Mother Earth are you doing?" I cried. Falcon did not flinch, but Solange and The Porcupine did.

J-B whispered loudly to me, "Be quiet, Keskoua. We can't have them hear us and come here."

"Sorry."

"No you aren't but you must remember we are not back on our own land. Our own safe land? Safe so far, at least."

"Sorry."

I glanced around at every corner. "Where is it? Where's my munti?"

"It's right here," said Matuwes, patting what looked like a pile of skins on the blanket beside her. She lifted it up and handed it to me.

"This is ALL?" I dropped to my knees and quickly opened the top to peer inside. "There's nothing left in here!"

"Keskoua. Hush."

"Where did it all go?"

Matuwes shrugged. "I needed some stuff out of it."

"Overnight? You've used up everything in here overnight?"

"Not everything. There's still a lot of stuff left in there."

She was right. Not everything had disappeared. But as I rummaged through my munti, I could find no ointment that would make the baby slippery enough to turn it and get it out of this girl. "I had ointment in here. Where did it go?"

Matuwes adjusted her body to get into a kneeling position. From there she was able to rise. She stood over me. "I needed it."

My teeth put pressure on my tongue.

"When I opened the package, and touched the ointment, it felt so good. It was so soft and smooth, I knew it would feel good on my feet. So I used it. Healers have to take care of themselves, too, you know."

"Do you know anywhere I can get goose fat?"

Matuwes's mouth fell open. "Is that what that stuff was made out of?" She looked down at her feet. "That's disgusting. By tomorrow I will stink."

"By tomorrow, this girl will be dead. And I have a good mind to tie her to you and you to her for at least a week afterwards to make you stink for the rest of your life."

The Porcupine's mouth closed and the bottom lip came out. "That's not very nice."

"Go see if you can find some."

"But don't you need my help?"

I shook my head. "Please. Go ask."

I was surprised, but Matuwes actually went away.

I told J-B to wait outside.

I hadn't noticed, but Agada was right beside me, quiet and even paler than I could ever have imagined she could get to be.

"The baby is stuck," she said. "Does it hurt, Solange? No, I'm sorry. That was a stupid question. Of course it must hurt." Her eyes looked into mine. "How can you fix it?"

"As you can see," I pointed to my munti. "I don't have very much to work with. Your new *healer* used up everything I had in it."

From the moaning pile of cedars and skins on the earthen floor of this strange shelter came Solange's weak voice. "She is no healer. She gave something to Falcon to make him sleep. She wants him for herself."

Something between a bark and a laugh came out of Agada. "She wants all of them for herself. But mostly Mak and Falcon. You should have heard her last night talking about you and Mak being away together all night."

"We never did anything together," came Solange's voice again. "We never did."

Did this girl expect me to believe her? Did she think I would be more likely to help her if I thought she hadn't been with my husband?

"Ohhhh! Can you please help me? Please. I beg of you. Get it out of me."

Agada leaned forward. To Solange she said, "I want to tell Keskoua something. We'll be right back." She stood up and grabbed one of my hands. "I have something to tell you."

I got up and let her lead me to Falcon where she lifted the skin blanket that was covering his legs.

Between his legs was a munti.

"See?"

Could I hope that some of the things I might need would be inside it? "Where did this come from?"

Agada's voice became a whisper. "Remember the healer I told you about? The one who was trying to help Solange?"

I nodded.

"That was hers. I snuck it in when Matuwes wasn't looking. She would have taken everything for herself. Like she did with yours."

I threw my arms around Agada. "You may have just saved your friend's life."

"And the life of your husband. And it's true, you know. He and Solange didn't do the... You know. They didn't do anything. He was faithful to you."

"But why did he let everyone think he was doing... the 'you know' with her?" I was finally able to smile at Agada who was seeming more relaxed right then. "Let's see what's inside this thing."

I opened it and was happy to learn that the healer who had tried to help Solange had thought the same way I did. From what I could tell, many of the things I would need were inside her munti.

Agada and I went back and knelt beside Solange.

"I am hoping you will be able to assist me with certain things that may not be pleasant. I hope it doesn't come to that, but it might." And I really meant what I said. The last thing I wanted to do, even though the baby was dead and already beginning to decay, was cut it out of its mother.

Agada swallowed.

Solange moaned.

I opened the package of what I knew would be ointment and took a deep breath.

Gasping from what I knew must be a most unbearable pain, Solange said, "If that doesn't work..." Her eyes went to Agada's face.

"Yes," said Agada. "I know. If that doesn't work, then we will do what we need to do. But we will do it with the greatest respect. Won't we, Keskoua?"

That we would.

Seventeen

W e quickly got all the medicines from the munti of Solange's healer into mine. There was enough ointment, and because it was made of the best ingredients, Agada and I were able to get the baby out of Solange without hurting her any more than we had to. And without cutting apart the baby.

We had no sooner cleaned up and had placed the remains of Solange's baby inside a large birch bark container that had been set aside for this exact purpose, when Matuwes entered the shelter with a handful of what was a far cry from being the goose fat I'd sent her for.

"Hope I'm not too late." She held out her hand. It had a grayish substance smeared on the palm.

Agada and I exchanged looks.

"Matuwes. That is not goose fat."

"What's your problem? It'll work fine. It's fish slime. Nice and slippery. See?"

I ignored her and wrapped my arms around the birch bark container that held Solange's baby and squeezed it close to my chest. "Wipe that disgusting substance off your hand then carry this—with respect—to somewhere it can be buried. Dig a hole. Then walk away. Agada will place it inside the hole and cover it. She has respect for the dead."

"Let her do it all then. I'm too old to be digging holes in the bush.

And you need me to help you with Falcon."

"Your help with Falcon is the last thing I need. And from what I understand, absolutely the last thing he needs."

I was surprised when Agada spoke up. "And after what Solange told me you did to her and her baby, I don't want to look at you." Agada turned her back to Matuwes.

This was a powerful message among our people and one we did not use often. I was surprised that Agada knew about it. Although she didn't have it quite right. We didn't turn our backs out of anger. When a member of our village did something very wrong, he was banished to the bush. No one was to speak to him—or her—until he was invited back by the Grandfathers and Grandmothers. If he approached us, we were to turn our backs on him. He was to spend his time alone. To do things on his own. To seek help and knowledge from the land itself.

Matuwes shrugged. "I was only trying to help. Nobody else around here was going to do it."

I wondered what exactly she had done to Solange, but I didn't ask. I'm not sure I wanted to know either. "Never mind all that right now. Go. Both of you. Take care of this dear wee soul." I handed the container to Agada. Matuwes still had fish slime on her hand. I pointed to it. "Rub your hands together and maybe the spirit of that long-dead fish will stop blisters from forming on your hands when you dig."

"You have no right to speak to me like this. I am your elder."

I moved my face close to hers. "I know a child who is only ten winters old that I consider to be my elder. You are not my elder. Now go."

Eighteen

With Solange's baby taken care of, I could now point my energies toward Falcon. But first, I had to go back to Mak's temporary village to collect kaksk´us, cedar, and a few other things I hoped I could more easily and quickly find there. The other healer's munti that Agada and Solange had hidden from Matuwes and given to me contained many things, the most important being a good amount of dried sage for the tea that would help dry up Solange's milk, to ease, at least, the pain in her breasts, but it had held no kaksk´us.

I had collected what I needed and was ready to head back through the swamp to the shelter when Bear approached me. "Are you absolutely certain you will be na to´q? I don't trust that woman one bit."

I didn't trust Matuwes either, but that wasn't going to stop me from trying to save Falcon's life. From what I had observed so far, she and I were at least in agreement on that. Or so it appeared on the outside of her.

I could put my trust in Agada, though. While working together to help Solange, she and I had quickly become as close friends as two people with entirely opposite views of life could. Her, I could trust. And I knew she would be with me, at my side, whenever Matuwes was around. That's how much I distrusted The Porcupine. I was afraid to be alone with her.

I didn't like to think in a bad way about Solange, but I was afraid of her, too. Women do have the sadness that comes and goes after a baby is born but if their baby dies, it adds more to their sadness and makes it stay longer. And it's a different kind of sadness. If the baby dies inside, the sadness becomes much worse. Other things can become worse, too, if the baby dies inside. The mother can go elue'wiet, crazy. Maybe even become dangerous. And I knew nothing of this grande vérole she suffered with. Or even if it made her suffer in the first place. What would a combination of extreme sorrow and this disease do to a person inside their head? No matter what, I doubted if she would be of any help to Agada and me while we tried to make Falcon wake up.

I got the idea that Agada was wanting to learn as much as she could about healing so I would do my best to help her learn as much as I could teach her in the time I had before going back to Port Royal and my own village. I would even ask her if she wanted to come back with me—with or without Second Son—so she could learn more. But right now, we had work to do. Hard work. We had to try to save Falcon's life and we had to keep The Porcupine out of the way to do it.

Right now, I was trying to concentrate on not forgetting anything before I left Mak's temporary village, but there was Bear at my elbow like a bee at a flower.

"They don't need you here, Bear. Flower Stalk needs your help there. In her temporary village. Not this temporary village. Mak has everything under control here. There are enough men and women, and they are well enough, to help with the dikes."

Behind him, I could see Mak on his knees, pretending not to pay attention to us while he adjusted the ropes that held several travoises and blankets together.

"See? He's getting your travois ready."

Without turning around, he said, "Yes. I see that."

"You'll be helping Flower Stalk and her people. That's a good thing to do, isn't it? I'm fine. Don't worry about me."

Bear's eyes then went from Mak to me then back to Mak.

One of the young Spirit Questers, who had been with J-B, already had his hands wrapped around the handles of a second travois with its own bundle of blankets and extra travoises. "Come on, Bear. We need to go get the rest of the bodies from Flower Stalk's village.

Bear's face was stern. "Are you certain you will be na to´q?"

"E´e."

"Promise me you won't try to follow us on your own when you've finished looking after Falcon."

I didn't say anything, I just dipped my head and looked up at him from under my raised eyebrows.

"Don't give me that look." He kissed my forehead before he stepped toward the bundle of travoises. "Or that one either." To Mak, he said, "You take care of her but don't be bringing her into any underground caves anymore." He bent down and picked up the handles of his loaded-down travois.

Mak's face did not change and even though I was looking at Bear's face from the side, I knew his face did not change either.

"Safe travels," I told him.

When I turned around, I nearly bumped into Agada who was holding a small pile of kaksk´us on the palm of her outstretched hand. "Is this right?"

"You found cedar, too?"

"Near the shelter. And I collected it like you told me." She tucked the cedar into a bag hanging across her chest from her shoulder, like my munti hangs from mine. It was the old healer's munti. She withdrew a piece of dried tobacco leaf. "I left a piece of this at the foot of the tree and said, 'Wela'lin, Grandmother Tree.'"

"And you found tobacco! Where did you get that?"

Her sly smile told me not to ask in front of everybody and she turned away. "Let's go. We have to hurry before she gets back. She was about to do something to him and he woke up a little bit. Then she saw me watching her and got into a fluster and ran out. If she knows I'm gone, he's in trouble. Solange is there but I don't know if she can fight her off or not. With my sister's mood the way it is, she might try. She already had a temper. But she would harm herself in doing so."

As I put the last of my own collection into my munti and hooked it over my shoulder, Agada grabbed me by the elbow and pulled. "Come on. We have to get there before she comes back."

She was stronger than she looked. I tripped and almost fell.

"Careful. But hurry."

As we made our way through the swamp, Agada asked, "Is it true that those with red hair are born with anger in them? Born with a temper?"

"I would be more willing to believe there are just people out there who are taught to fear those who are different from themselves and their own people, so must blame their fears on something else."

"I think I'm going to believe that, too. It makes more sense."

***

We were too late. By the time we had splashed our way through the salty water to the strange island made of logs, Matuwes was already bending over Falcon, and Solange, with water coming out of her forehead, was crumpled on the floor beside them, trying her best to pull Matuwes away from Falcon, but her arms kept falling down.

Much too weak to resist, Solange allowed Agada to guide her back to her pile of skins. From there, she whimpered, "Tell her to stop. She did the same to me. Tell her to stop."

Matuwes had placed a long tube, made out of some kind of plant stem, down Falcon's throat. Using a spoon, and her hand as a funnel, she was pouring a reddish-brown liquid into the plant stem.

As quickly as I could, I lifted the strap of my munti over my head and almost threw it toward Agada. Agada was not only strong, she was quick, too. She caught it.

I reached down and ripped the plant stem from Falcon's throat and flipped it away. I grabbed Matuwes by the back of her head, by her hair, and leaned her face up to me. I had never felt such rage inside me. "How dare you. How dare you pour something down anyone's throat let alone someone who is not awake."

Matuwes's eyes once again became those of a chenoo. "You think you know everything. There is nothing better for him. I have been giving it to him for days. Look at him. He is still alive."

A groan from Solange in the far corner of the shelter.

"What is it?" I demanded. I let go of Matuwes's hair.

She rubbed the back of her head. "I paid well for it."

"I said, what is it?"

Agada closed in behind me. "It's called 'law do numb,' or something like that. She gets it from a Portuguese sailor."

Matuwes licked the hand that had been guiding the liquid into Falcon.

"Laudanum? Is that true, Matuwes? You've been giving laudanum to Falcon?"

"Bottles of it," added Agada. "Little brown bottles. That's one there." Agada pointed to Falcon's chest where a small brown bottle and several other objects lay.

These disappeared into a bag that had been laying on the floor and in an instant, Matuwes was on her feet and backing up beyond the length of my arms, with her hands, and the bag, behind her.

Agada, hair out of the way, exposing those strange, pale eyes, moved to the far end of Falcon's cot. "Yes. That's it. That's what it's called. Every time that sailor came to port, she would disappear into the bush with him." She straightened out the skins that were covering Falcon. Then, head high, she faced Matuwes. "He would come out all smiles. She would come out with funny-looking eyes. I know what that's all about. She's taking that medicine, too. Aren't you?"

"You're a liar, foreign witch."

Agada turned to me then. "What is it? How dangerous is it? Is she going to die, too? I don't like her but I don't want anybody to die."

"She'll be fine. Won't you, Matuwes?" I pointed my head toward Solange and made my eyes big at Agada. "And nobody's going to die. Are they?"

Agada's hair slipped down to hide her face again. "Sorry."

I immediately bent over the sleeping Falcon to lift, first, one eyelid, then the other. The dark round circles in the middle of his eyes were small. "Thank you for the information, Agada. You may have saved Falcon's life. And you have already saved Solange's life." I glanced over at Solange. "Isn't that right, Solange?"

Solange managed to squeeze out a smile that came from both her mouth and her eyes. A good sign. She would get better fast. A lot faster than Falcon would.

To Matuwes I said, "I want to know why you were giving him such a dangerous substance."

A grunt.

"I have heard it gives pleasure to those who use it, so I understand why you might want it for yourself. But to give it to someone who can't wake up is…"

I didn't wait for an answer. I motioned for Agada to give me my munti. She set it between Falcon's feet and opened it for me. I searched inside to find my listening device which I held to Falcon's chest. As I suspected, I could hear gurgling. His lungs were full of liquid.

I put my listening device back into my munti and said to Agada, "We have to get him turned over onto his stomach to drain his lungs. They are full."

"I was aware of that," said Matuwes. "That's why I was giving him the medicine. They counteract each other. Don't you know anything?"

A weak laugh came from Solange's side of the shelter.

Hearing Solange laugh made me feel good but not by a lot. I didn't dare speak another word to Matuwes. I needed to use my energy to help Falcon, and not attack her and force the rest of the bottle down *her* throat which was exactly what I wanted to do right then.

Between Agada and me, we were able to roll Falcon over so the top half of him was hanging off the cot. We placed smooth blankets under his head and covered him with bearskins.

"There now. We can leave him like that for a while, but if his face starts turning red by too much—"

"I can do that," came Solange's weak voice. "Let me do that. I can watch him."

"Good idea, Solange. Yes, please watch him. If that happens. If he goes red—and he will—we have to put him back on the cot. But on his side. On one side, then on the other side. You understand, Agada? Back and forth many times a day?"

"Every hour maybe?"

"Yes. Every hour."

"I don't have a watch but I know what an hour is."

"When he does wake up, he will be suffering with many things."

If I had looked at myself the way I was now glaring at Matuwes, I would have run away screaming, terrified, out onto the land. I was enraged that he would have to experience the stages of getting the laudanum out of himself on top of having lungs full of water. It was all Matuwes's doing. I couldn't help myself.

Her shoulders went up and her head went to one side.

To Agada and Solange, I said, "He won't be able to sleep. He will have pain in his body. Water may run out of his skin. And he may become afraid or angry when he wakes up."

"You mean like poor Solange?" The water in Agada's eyes was getting ready to spill out.

"Worse. Way worse."

Matuwes laughed. "*If* he wakes up, you mean. I'm telling you, he needs the laudanum."

"How much have you been giving him, Matuwes? And how often? And since when? Since the moment he was drowned? You are a fool. He should have been placed like this, upside down, right away."

"That's not what Caetano told me. Caetano told me to—"

"And you trusted him. You trusted a man with… What's that word? Ah, yes. You trusted a man with ulterior motives. One who has trained you as though you are his pet squirrel."

"I—"

"Yes, you."

A gurgling made all four of us look at the blankets under Falcon's head.

Solange pointed and cried out. "Look. There's something coming out of him already!"

A brownish-green foaming substance spread outward on the blankets below his mouth.

Agada gasped. "That's a good thing, yes? Please tell me that's a good thing."

"It is, Agada. It is."

With a relieved sigh, Solange flopped back against her pile of skins and blankets.

"That's disgusting," said Matuwes. "That's what Caetano told me I had to avoid at all costs."

"Only if you were trying to kill him."

"App?"

"It looks like your lover was trying to eliminate the competition. Right, Agada?"

"He wouldn't do that."

An understanding smile spread across Agada's face. "You're really stupid sometimes, Matuwes. Even stupider than me and Solange thought you were. You're even stupider than we are."

A laugh and a "*Hej!*" came from Solange.

Solange's dark, sad, angry mood was beginning to rise away from her like morning mist from a lake. I was relieved and happy about that.

"Don't ever say that about yourself." I pointed my thumb at Matuwes. "About her, it's na to´q, though."

"App?"

A smile crawled onto my face. Yes, I was getting over my anger. Anger was something that couldn't rest in me longer than a handful of snow on a rock in a Sacred Fire. It could be as fierce as a fire when it came out of me, but it was always gone in its own mist.

"But it's not na to´q about you or Solange. Promise me?"

"Promise me, too," laughed Solange.

I was beginning to like her. A lot.

Agada's soft, accepting face warmed my heart more than I could have ever imagined. "I promise."

"What did you say about me? I demand an apology."

Nineteen

It took nearly two days to get the liquids from the sea out of Falcon's lungs, but it would take much longer for him to wake up from the poison Matuwes had been forcing into him. If he woke up at all. I knew he had been drinking a lot of alcohol every day, so would have already gone through something getting that out of himself, too, but that would have happened when he was asleep with the laudanum. I couldn't believe he was still alive until I reminded myself that this was Falcon. Falcon, the man who could do almost anything.

Solange was, by now, feeling better physically, too, and had offered to help, so she and Agada said they would look after him while I returned to Mak's village then to Flower Stalk's village to help them pull the bodies out of the bay. I knew these young women would follow my instructions because they liked Falcon, so would do everything in their power to keep Matuwes from trying to hurt him again. Whether I stayed or went back to help Flower Stalk would make no difference to Falcon. It wasn't just his lungs. He didn't know any of us and didn't know where he was. I wanted to believe it was because he was coming out of the poison fog but knew deep down that his brain was hurt from not breathing for too long.

Before I left, I had to make sure that Agada and Solange had enough food and enough medicines in Agada's munti to keep them going until I got back.

We needed to get food and Matuwes seemed to be the only one who knew where some might be.

"I need your help, Matuwes," I told her.

"Oh. So now she needs me. For what?"

"Where were your people's three sisters planted? Or did the Maudits anglaises destroy that area, too?"

"Sisters?" Solange frowned.

"Sisters, but not like us," laughed Agada.

"Oh. Now I remember. Their three sisters are corn, squash and beans that climb up the corn. The squash grows around on the ground around them. They help each other out."

"Like us."

"Like us."

"Sisters."

"Sisters."

"We need berries, too," I said. "Where did those berries come from? The ones they had the other day at Mak's temporary village."

The smile on the face of Matuwes made a squirrel run up my back.

"*You* know. Don't you?" I demanded.

"What will you give me if I show you?"

Agada, who now was keeping her hair tied up with a ribbon made from cedar bark, stepped forward into the face of Matuwes. "Your question should be what will we give *you* if you *don't* show us?"

"Even if I told you, there's no way we can cook any of it so why bother?"

"One step at a time. Step one? Show us!"

Agada's words that close to Matuwes made her wipe her face.

"Help us get the food. We'll figure out what to do with it then. Remember, we aren't stupid."

"Very well. I'll take Keskoua with me and show her."

"I will go with you," said Agada.

Matuwes turned her face away but not before I saw the chenoo in it. "We can't leave Solange alone. Can we?"

"I'm feeling much stronger." Solange raised one arm and pointed at the muscle on it with her other hand.

Agada hugged her and said, "You won't be able to turn Falcon over by yourself. Even with me and Keskoua working together, it's hard to do."

Solange hung her head then raised it again. "Tell the boy outside to go get somebody."

"What boy," I asked.

Agada and Solange exchanged smiles but Matuwes was the one who spoke. "Spies. He has spies everywhere watching you."

"Only three," came a voice from outside the shelter. "Me and two others." A face came around the corner of one of the moss-covered logs. It was one of J-B's Spirit Questers. "I'm Little Bat."

"You can help her then," said Agada.

"I'm not allowed to enter your shelter. That was specific."

"Are you allowed to leave? To go ask them to send help?"

"There's nobody there. They're all gone. They are either helping Flower Stalk or preparing the dikes for installation as soon as Sun goes away. Remember? And Sun will be going away soon."

"Well then there's nobody who will tell on you if you come in to help Solange, is there?"

His face told me he wasn't going to listen to me, either.

"Orders are orders." Little Bat stuck his chin out.

"Will you at least go ask Mak what to do?" I was getting impatient with this boy's integrity. "We'll wait."

"One of *you* go ask."

"Who? Her? We trust her?" I pointed at Matuwes.

"That makes at least ten apologies you owe me now," she grumbled.

"Want to make it eleven?" I shot back.

Face squashed into itself like a dried-up blueberry, Matuwes stepped toward me, fist raised.

A shadow appeared beside Little Bat. A tall shadow. It was Mak.

"I'll take over from here, Little Bat. Take a break."

Twenty

Little Bat was right. Sun was getting low in the sky and this would make it darker and darker, not good for walking through unknown bush. But we had no choice, the tide was now out. I quickly grabbed a few pieces of dried cow and some birch bark, wrapped these in more birch bark and tucked everything into my munti. This would do for the three of us until we got to where we were going—wherever that was—but I hoped Matuwes was telling the truth, that the three sisters would still be there so we would have enough food to get us back to the shelter. We all carried empty bags, and our own water, too. Agada also had her new munti. She was proud of it.

I adjusted the bags on my shoulders. "Ready."

Matuwes elbowed me to the side and strode away.

"Uh. Matuwes?" Mak's voice came from behind us. He was pointing to another area of the clearing edge where a huge boulder sat.

She turned to face it.

"You can't take the old path. Remember? You can connect to the new one from behind that boulder. It goes through the swamp for a short dis—"

"Oh. Of course. Of course. Thank you. I'm under such stress, it's hard to keep everything straight. Thank you, Mak. You're always so very kind to me."

I waved my hand at Solange who waved back, and I smiled at Mak who didn't return the smile. But Little Bat did. Yes. Little Bat smiled at me, at Mak then back at me. I swear, there's nothing worse than people talking about each other and spreading stories that aren't true.

***

Most paths through the bush are like an old Talking Stick, massaged smooth over years of gentle use, but the path I was now following The Porcupine through was narrow and sharp, recently cut open like a fish from the wrong side of it, through its bones.

We spoke quietly.

"When is the last time you went through here, Matuwes?"

"Shortly ago."

From behind me, a laugh from Agada. "I go through here with Secky every few days and I have yet to see you anywhere near here."

"Are you accusing me of something?"

"I think you accuse yourself every time you open your mouth."

"Secky?"

"Oh, sorry, Keskoua. Second Son."

"Ah, yes. Do you think he'll ever ask for another name than Second Son?"

Matuwes muttered something I couldn't quite hear so I asked her to say it again. She did. "I'm sure he would only want another name if it had the word Chief attached to it."

"While we are speaking of names, who gave you the name Porcupine?"

"Nobody. I did."

"Why? To make people think you could hurt them before they hurt you? Good name to keep men from sneaking up behind you. Right?"

I tried to make that a joke but from the way Matuwes's shoulders went tight, I knew I had made a mistake.

"You are mostly Acadian, though. You must have had a baptism name. What was it?"

"I don't know."

I'd heard that before but couldn't quite remember where or when, but then, behind me, Agada spoke up. "Like Dit Ça. He was away with them, too, and can't remember his real name. At least, that's what someone told me."

"Ah. Yes. I heard that. I heard it from him himself. When I first arrived, Flower Stalk's people had a Sacred Fire. The man who is called Dit Ça spoke of a girl they called Dit Ceci. Is that you, Matuwes?"

"She doesn't talk about those times."

"I don't talk about those times. I don't want that mi´jan in my head."

"You need it in your head to get it out of your head or it will make you sick everywhere else in your body. Buried memories eat you like worms eat a buried body. They will end up everywhere inside you if you don't bring them into your head and out of your mouth."

Agada's voice, "But what if thinking about them causes other problems?"

"Did the Grandmothers want to give you another name?"

"I don't know. I like the one I have. I did not ask, and I will not ask for another."

"Ah. So that's why you understand Second Son so well?"

"That's not even the slightest bit funny and you know it," Matuwes snapped back at me then suddenly went to her knees. "Hush!"

Her free arm shot out to wave me into the trees.

Agada followed.

We crouched there, afraid to breathe.

Matuwes crawled in beside us.

I used my lips and only the slightest wind from inside me to ask her. "What did you see?"

"A soldier. A guard. See him?"

Through the trees, we were able to see a patch of green that was solid, not like leaves.

"It's a Maudits anglais?"

"I think so."

From the other side of me, Agada whispered. "I can see his face. I know him. It's all right." She rose to her feet and stepped out of the trees.

"Moqwa´! No, no. Don't."

She spoke in English. "Hey, Hammy. It's me. Agada. Don't shoot me." She laughed. "How are you?"

Agada disappeared, but I could hear their voices.

A male voice, young, Hammy, said, "Agada. What a pleasant surprise. Where is… Where is *he*?"

"Not with me today."

"Ah. See? Blessings do come along on occasion. But what are you doing here? Are you alone?"

"I have two ladies with me. Respected ladies. Important ladies."

"Where are they then?"

"Hiding."

Laughter.

Then Agada's voice, "Come out from there, Keskoua. Matuwes, it's all right. You can come out. He's not going to shoot you."

I helped Matuwes to her feet and we cautiously went toward Agada and the guard.

"Come on, come on." Agada waved to us. "He's not going to do anything to you. But don't tell Second Son that."

She and Hammy exchanged glances that held secrets.

"I'm Keskoua."

"Abraham. She calls me Hammy."

Agada giggled. "Because he likes to eat pork."

"Doesn't everyone?"

I continued with the introductions. "This is Matuwes. She used to live in the village that's… I haven't been there for many years so don't know exactly where it is. More like where it used to be. It was around here somewhere."

"I know it. You are right. It's not far. I can take you there."

Agada hooked her arm through the arm that didn't hold Hammy's musket. "That would be wonderful. Come on, ladies. Follow us."

It was now my turn to exchange glances, with Matuwes. "You look as bewildered as I am."

Her eyebrows went together.

"Bewildered? It means confused. I've wanted to use the word 'bewildered' since the first time I read it in one of Marguerite's books."

Her eyebrows stayed where they were.

"She gets books from Boston. All the time. She lends them to me to read."

"Ah." Matuwes relaxed and followed behind Hammy and Agada. "Who is Marguerite?"

"She's the wife of my friend Claude Guidry. They are J-B's parents."

"Ah."

I was glad to finally have the chance to use that word out loud. But I think I would be needing a stronger word for "bewildered" soon, because when Agada told us how she and Hammy had become friends, I was more than bewildered.

On one of their trips to the village where Matuwes and Mak and the others had lived, Second Son had discovered a "still."

"What's a still?"

Hammy explained it to Matuwes and me. "It's where they make whiskey. And no, our people did not fire any cannon at the area once we discovered its existence." He chuckled. "I'm surprised you don't know about it. What good is growing wheat in such abundance if you don't turn some of it into whiskey?"

"Is this why Second Son decided to 'help' everyone in this area?" I asked Agada.

"Not at first. No. But when he learned about it, he thought of it as a gift from Mother Earth for helping them."

"And he learned about it how?"

"Through devious means," Hammy said. "Second Son ordered Agada to comfort me."

Agada touched her side, the side with the sore ribs. I don't think she realized she did it.

"She was to extract information. About our military plans."

"Quel cochon." This, from Matuwes. *What a pig.*

"I know that word. And I agree. But I am newly wed and love my wife beyond anything. I would not ever risk my marriage like that. But we had to go along with him. He was in one of his… What do you call them?"

"In one of his *stemninger*. One of his moods."

"Yes. One of his moods. So we went into the forest."

"And made appropriate sounds."

"And then discussed what information I could reveal that would satisfy him."

"He told me about the still."

"You don't have to tell me any more than that," I laughed.

"And the best thing about that," said Agada, once more smiling with affection at Hammy, "was that they didn't shoot cannons at the three sisters either. They're all safe."

"Not all of them," Hammy added. "We have been using them for ourselves."

Matuwes clapped her hands. "What wonderful news. What wonderful news."

"See, Keskoua? I told you she was lying about coming back here."

"I don't lie. I demand an apology."

Twenty-one

Hammy was kind enough to guide us to a clearing near the three sisters area where we could make tea, catch our breath and have something to eat. We didn't have much to eat except for, as I said, dried cow, birch bark to chew on and the few berries we had collected along the way, so he shared his rations with us. His rations were mostly from our own three sisters—corn, beans and squash—so were welcomed by all three of us, even though they weren't cooked according to our traditional ways.

After we had refreshed ourselves, we went to collect our own corn, beans and squash. Agada showed me where she had found the tobacco. There wasn't much but it was good to have even a little bit. Hammy showed us the still, which was mostly underground because, as he told us, part of the process needed the tubes to be cold. The stench of the area kept me away from it, but Matuwes and Agada came out of the hole in the ground with bottles of whiskey in their arms and smiles on their faces.

Agada handed one to me. "I think your friend Pierre would like this? As a special treat? Perhaps even a bribe. A reward for something."

I slid the bottle into my munti. "I will find a use for it."

As Agada handed another of the bottles to Hammy, he told us he would be going back to his ship until the next day. That another guard would be replacing him. A guard who liked nothing better than to capture female prisoners.

Again, his kindness glowed like Sun peeking over the horizon on a clear morning. He showed us another area where we would be safe until the next day when he returned. It was a cabin, crushed and cracked from cannon shot, but it held blankets and skins and a stove like Marguerite and Claude had at their cabin. The three remaining walls had fallen in on each other to provide a place safe from rain and spying eyes. Any smoke from the stove would be hidden from any ship's eyes by hills and trees. We would leave early next morning at low tide.

**

I can't describe to you what it felt like to have a full belly after going so many days without one. All three of us lay back on the blankets and skins and breathed in the night's air with pleasure.

We had used the stove to cook our meals and now the dying embers gave off a soothing warmth.

Matuwes was the first to speak.

"I'm going to try to talk about it. Like you said I should." She sat up and crossed her legs.

"I'll make you a promise," said Agada. "If you do, I will." She, too, sat up and crossed her legs.

"Wait," I said, rising to my feet. "I'll go out and find a stick."

"In the dark?" laughed Agada. "You do have special powers, oh great healer."

"No need." Matuwes, with great respect, waved a little branch. "Do we sit around the stove? And pretend it's a Sacred Fire?"

Agada and I smiled at each other then at Matuwes. We spoke at the same time. "You decide."

We adjusted ourselves as Matuwes leaned forward to open the grate in the front of the stove to let the glowing coals spread their light out onto our faces.

"Yes," Matuwes began. "Dit Ça and I know each other. And well. We were both taken from our parents when we were young. Put on a ship and dumped like a sack of grain on the docks of Boston Harbor. From there we were taken to a distant village and a huge building with many small rooms in it. Some with no windows.

"Our clothing was removed and they made us rub coal tar all over our bodies. Especially our hair, they told us. And they struck the ones who didn't do it right, with switches. Then we were forced into tubs of cold water. All the way under." She shivered. "The soap they gave us burned our skin. They gave us new clothing. Clothing that was tight and uncomfortable and layer upon layer and the collar around my neck made me feel like I was always choking. They covered our hair. After they cut most of it off."

I must have gasped because Agada said, "What's wrong? Solange cut hers off. Is that bad?"

I told her, "We cut our hair only when we are in mourning. Our hair is sacred."

"I was in mourning, all right. I've never been so sad in my life. At least that's what I thought at the time. I didn't think it could get worse."

"Were there men there?" asked Agada.

"I know why you are asking that question, dear girl. And the answer is yes. And yes, they did."

Agada got up off her blanket and crossed over to sit beside Matuwes. She put both arms around her and held her so tightly, I thought Matuwes would not be able to breathe. But Matuwes's eyes closed and I saw a tear drop out of the one closest to me onto Agada's head.

"You understand, don't you?" Agada said.

"I do."

"And that's why you named yourself Porcupine."

"Yes."

"I'm so sorry for saying all those mean things to you."

"I think we're even on that account. I said many things about you when you and Second Son showed up in our temporary village. I hated you because you are beautiful. And also, because you had a man." Matuwes pushed Agada back and stared into her eyes. "Even though it's only Second Son." She laughed.

Agada laughed.

My teeth closed on my tongue.

"Did you find it difficult to learn their language?" I asked. "I know J-B has a difficult time with speaking English. He speaks everything else."

"In his case, I think desire is involved. He has no wish to speak the language of the Maudits anglaises. In my case, I had no choice. Every time, every single time, even in my nightmares, if a French or Mi´gmaw word slipped out of me, the switch was applied to my back. I was called a devil."

She smiled at me. "Thank you, Keskoua. There is much to remember but releasing even this much has helped me. It really has. There was only one man, really. One who actually... actually..."

"Penetrated you?" This came from Agada.

Matuwes hung her head.

"Do not be ashamed. The one thing I learned from Second Son..." and here, Agada turned to me. "He's not all bad, you know. There is some kindness and wisdom in him."

"E´e. I know."

"Things happened to him as a child, too."

"I did not know this."

"It is not up to me to tell you, though. It has to come from him. E´e?"

"E´e."

"But this about him will be about me so I can say it. The best thing I learned from him is to never feel ashamed for what others did to me. I did not choose. They chose. Not me."

Matuwes handed the little stick to Agada. "This isn't working the way it should. We're all talking and it's supposed to be just me." She laughed. "But maybe it will help you open up, too? Would you like to share with us? What your life was like? Is like?"

"I'll try." Agada caressed the stick. "Solange and I are sisters. Believe it or not." She brushed at her pale-yellow hair. "She is older by one year. Our mother was Irish. That's where her red hair came from. I don't know where my white hair came from. It's called albinism. And I don't know where my albinism came from. But both of our hair cursed us to be always in the eyes of somebody." She glanced over at Matuwes.

"Sorry," said Matuwes.

"It caused the death of our father."

Right at that moment, something in the woodstove snapped. It was only a piece of wood letting an air pocket escape from it, but it made all of us jump.

"Should I take that as a message?" I didn't know if Agada was making a joke or if she was truly frightened. I didn't know her well enough yet.

"It's only the wood releasing its spirit. Did it scare you?"

Her smile told me she was teasing me. Or, perhaps, she was trying to make herself feel happy about what she was going to tell us.

"Carry on," said Matuwes. "You will feel better. I did. I do. And I shared only a small portion of what's inside me."

"Very well. Men were wanting us. We were no longer in Ireland, you see. We had gone with Father to Denmark for work. In Ireland, Father was known for his ability to grow almost anything and they needed someone like him there. And also, he had done something in Ireland that the authorities didn't like. I never did find out what it was, but I don't think it took much to have the authorities get their eyes on you at that time. I think it was his success that condemned him.

"Anyway. We moved to Denmark. Where the problems ended up being worse. They found something to be angry with Father about so he, like many others, was sent away into the military. They did that a lot. And that's how he got killed. At least, that's what we were told. Mother could not survive on her own, so soon, we had a stepfather."

Here, Agada shuddered and her breathing became shallow and fast.

Matuwes rubbed her arm. "You can stop."

"No, I can't. This man. This stepfather… He loaned us out in exchange for food and drink."

"What about your mother? What did she do? Did she not try to stop him?"

"Once. And he beat her so badly, she forgot we were her daughters. Her mind became damaged."

"Like what happened to Dit Ça? I was there when they did that to him. I didn't think he was ever going to wake up. Was it the same with your mother?"

"For three days she didn't wake up. When she did, he did not give her water, he gave her Akvavit. Or beer. We always had more than enough of that in the house. Solange—when he was gone outside—would give her water. But we were too small to reach the cupboards and the stove to make food for her. Or for us, either. We didn't know how to do more than shell peas. Or tear up stale bread for stuffing partridges and chickens. When we had any. And there were no peas to shell. And, of course, we knew nothing of healing anyone. We were too young to know anything about anything."

I didn't want to know but I asked anyway. "How old were you?"

"I was seven, so Solange was eight."

Twenty-two

As we walked along the path back to the shelter early next morning, back to Falcon and back to Solange—and Mak, yes, back to Mak—Matuwes began to point out plants and trees to Agada. Most of the time, she was wrong about what they were, and worse, wrong about the way to use them.

"Where did you get your information about our plants and medicines?" I finally asked her, as kindly as I was able to. It wasn't easy. I was afraid I would make her become angry again and turn into herself and against what was outside of her. Like me, for one.

"Observation and training. No doubt the same way you did." It seemed Matuwes *was* back to her old self, a mui´n in the spring, a bear: hungry and impatient with everything.

"The healer who was killed—"

"Marianne," offered Agada.

"Marianne was teaching you? Is that where you learned?"

"What are you accusing me of?"

"Nothing. I'm asking. I—"

Agada spoke up. "I can tell you what I heard."

"Never repeat what you heard unless it's from the mouth of the person it's about. Lutmaqan, gossip, destroys both the teller and the one told about."

"How does anybody find out anything, then?"

"Good question, Agada. Do you have an answer for that, Keskoua? Oh great storyteller?"

"There's no need to be rude, Matuwes."

She shrugged. "She wouldn't tell me anything. I sneaked around behind her and watched."

"So you never learned any reasons why or why not."

A sad laugh escaped Matuwes. "Most of what I learned was why not."

I reached ahead to take hold of Matuwes's arm. "Let's stop and take a rest."

Agada was already on the ground. "Good idea." She was digging around in one of her bags. "Anyone care for a sweet?"

Both Matuwes and I spoke at the same time. "A sweet?"

"Yes. Hammy gave me some. Before we left this morning. He is such a kind man. He told me they might give us strength on the way back. I envy his wife."

"He was here? I mean there?"

"He sneaked in to give me the sweets. But that was just an excuse, really."

I sat on one side of Agada, and Matuwes sat on the other. We popped the sweets into our mouths.

"He wanted to give me information." Here, her voice went to a low whisper. "About Captain KrommeZee. They found out where he hides the ships he builds."

"That's not good, is it?" Matuwes asked me. Then she asked Agada, "Do they know where he builds them?"

"Just where he hides them."

Matuwes was on her feet and bounding along the rough path like a startled lentug, deer. "Come on. Come on. We must get this information to the others. We need to send a message to the captain."

Agada and I were right behind her.

To Agada, between breaths, I said, "This *is* information you 'hear' that you pass on to others immediately. But remember, never information that Marie Duck told Marie Fish told Marie Clam told Marie Toad. Na to´q?"

It felt good to make Agada laugh. I think it made her feel good, too. Even though it's difficult to do when running through rough and unfamiliar bush.

"Do you ladies mind? We're in a hurry here. We can't be wasting our breath on trivialities."

Twenty-three

W e had to stop to rest two times on the way back to the shelter, but that was only to take water and chew on a piece of birch bark. It wasn't far, but the path was difficult. It was shortly after Sun had reached the top of the sky that we came out from behind the big boulder.

I heard an apalqaqamej, a chipmunk, cry out *chook, chook, chook,* but I knew it was not a real chipmunk.

I called out, *caw, caw, caw, caw, caw.* Five caws. *All is well.*

Matuwes called out three, *caw, caw, caw. I agree.*

"Mak!" It was Little Bat's voice. "They're back. It's na to´q. It's them."

Matuwes burst into the shelter where she threw her arms around Mak, then around a surprised and reluctant Solange. She set her bags down on a blanket. "Captain KrommeZee. Tell me where he is. We have information. Important information."

Behind her, Agada and Solange exchanged hugs.

Mak hugged me even more briefly than the hug between him and Matuwes had lasted. His hug to Agada was kind and strong, like a father would give to a much-loved child.

"We have news, Kes—" Mak began.

Matuwes interrupted him. "We need to send someone to warn Captain KrommeZee. They know where he hides his ships. We have to warn him."

Matuwes bent down to open one of her bags. She withdrew three food packages and handed them to Agada. "Give these to that boy out there. One for him and two for the others. Think of it, Mak. Even if we had pigeons to send out, they would be of no use. They'd merely shoot them down." She handed a package to Solange, then one to Mak. "And no doubt they'd read the messages on them after. These are, believe it or don't believe it, a courtesy from the enemy." She handed Solange another package. "For Falcon," she said. Then one to Agada. "But I made the bannock. One of the Maudits anglaises has made friends with our young Agada here."

Agada and Solange exchanged knowing glances.

Matuwes paused to catch her breath. "Am I missing anything, Agada?"

Mak scratched at his chin. "I have to say I don't know where his ships are or where he builds them. Oh. Do they know where he builds them?"

"No," replied Agada. "Not yet, at least. They're looking. But Hammy told me they aren't looking as hard these days. Colonel Church has returned to New England. Most of the ships have returned, too."

"There are still ships in the harbor," I said.

"There's only one now," said Agada.

"And you believe this man?" Mak took an angry step toward Agada. "How much information did you give *him*?"

I expected Agada to curl away in fear but she did not. Instead, she pushed on Mak's chest. "Do not speak to me in that manner. I got information. True information. If you don't want to take advantage of it and—"

"You out there. Young man," Matuwes called out. "Do you know where Captain keeps his new ships?"

Little Bat made his face appear from around the corner of one of the logs. He was chewing on a piece of bannock. "Am I allowed to tell, Chief Mak?"

Mak's eyes pierced into my eyes, then Agada's eyes, then into the eyes of The Porcupine. "Can I trust you? Can I really trust you?"

"With my life," said Agada.

"With mine, too," I added.

Solange was busy eating what her sister had given her, but she nodded.

"There's no reason to distrust us, Mak," said Matuwes. "Listen. You don't need to tell us where they are or where Captain is. If the boy knows, just send him."

Mak smiled. "I don't understand you at all, Matuwes. You hide your wisdom from everyone, it seems, except from me. What are you afraid of by letting your true self show?"

"More than anyone knows," I said. "Let's not get into… What do they call it? Philosophical discussion?"

Everyone, even Solange, who had a mouthful of bannock in the background, said "App?"

"Never mind. Does the boy know?"

"The boy knows. Yes."

"Will you send him?"

"Little Bat?"

"Chief?"

"Will you go find Captain and tell him they know where he hides his new ships?"

"Of course, I will. It would be an honor to deliver such information."

"Is there anything else he needs to tell KrommeZee?"

"Not that I can think of," Agada said.

"Then off you go, young man."

"Wait. Wait," Agada pulled a sweet out of her bag and gave it to him. Before she let go of it into his hand, she asked. "May I ask you a question?"

"Sure."

"How do you know where the captain is?"

"Marie told me."

Matuwes, Agada and I laughed. This made Mak's eyebrows raise up and those of Solange squeeze together.

Agada continued, "Marie, uh? Which Marie? Was it Marie Duck, Marie Fish, Marie Clam or Marie Toad?"

Laughter came from Matuwes and me.

"App?" came from Little Bat.

"Never mind," said Matuwes. "Run along. And thank you. Be careful. And we'll see you back at Mak's village, e´e?"

"E´e." And off he went running, calling out to the other two Spirit Questers, "I am on a mission and you're not."

"All right. That's done," I said. "Let's get some food into Falcon and then we can relax." I stepped toward the cot where Falcon lay but Mak grabbed my arm.

"Uh…"

I hadn't noticed her move, but Solange was at my other side. She was wiping her mouth off with her sleeve. "I'm sorry, Keskoua. I'm so sorry. We did everything we could."

"App? What are you telling me? What are you saying?" I pushed them out of the way to get closer to Falcon.

I didn't have to touch him to know he would be cold and his body would feel like skin-covered stone. I knew he was dead.

"When did this happen?"

"We tried everything," said Solange. "We truly did."

"We did. She's telling you the truth." Mak took my arm again to keep me away from my husband.

"I said *when*. *When* did this happen?"

"Keskoua?" This from Matuwes who was behind me now. She gently nudged Solange away and took my other arm, trying to help Mak get me away from Falcon.

"NO!" I jabbed both elbows out into them and struggled away from their grasp. I went to him. I knelt beside him. I touched him. He was cold. He was stiff.

"During the night. Before dawn," Mak said quietly. "It sounded like he was choking on something. Right, Solange?"

"Like he was choking on something. Yes. That describes it perfectly."

"We sat him up."

"That's right. We did. There had been no foam coming out of him for a whole day so we weren't hanging him off the cot anymore."

"We moved him though. Like you said."

"Yes. From side to side. Every hour."

"Like you said."

"But then." Solange placed her hand on my shoulder. "But then he made another sound."

I knew what she was going to say. "Like something rattling."

"Yes."

Mak put his hand on my other shoulder. "Come on, Keskoua. We have to prepare for the ceremony. Don't we?"

I rose to my feet. Then, with every bit of power in me, I struck out with my fist at Mak's chest.

He stopped my hand and then pulled me into his arms where he held me until I stopped struggling. The way he held me was not only to comfort me and protect me from hurting myself, but my mouth was trapped into his shoulder so that's where my screams would die, unheard by anyone except for me and Mak. "*You* did it," I screamed into his flesh. "*You* killed him. *You* killed my husband. You and Solange."

There's time in here that I have lost and don't think I will ever recover because the next thing I knew, I was sitting there, wrapped in skins and blankets, and smelling sage burning and hearing the whimpers of Solange and Agada behind me. I think Matuwes had her arm around me. I could see through my swollen eyes that Mak was walking around Falcon and using an eagle feather to brush smoke on him.

"I didn't even look at him when I came in here."

"There were important things going on. Things that will save many lives."

"But he is—was—my husband. It's all my fault."

Solange: "No. It's my fault."

Mak: "It's his fault. We are never responsible for another's decisions. Life is all about choices. He made his. This is where his choices led him. Sorry, Keskoua. I don't mean to sound…"

"It's na to´q, Mak. I'm na to´q."

"No you aren't."

Twenty-four

I was able to sip tea, but the thought of food made my stomach promise to throw it back out. I didn't think I was still crying, but water kept dripping from my face, so I guess I was.

"We tried to feed Falcon with what we had but he wasn't able to chew anything, or even swallow when I cut it up real small." Solange hung her head. "He didn't exactly choke but we thought something was stuck there. It wasn't anything though. There was nothing in there. I know because I didn't put anything in there. He fluttered his eyes and stopped breathing. I don't think it was about the choking. He was still making that sound in his throat, that rattling, you said, so air was getting in and out. I think his brain shut everything down."

"It's time for us to wrap him in skins," said Mak. "May I? And to take him home?"

This made Solange's breathing go faster and faster and her bottom jaw quiver. Between gasps, "Sorry. I know the word in your language, so I will say it that way, too, Keskoua. I am mesgei´. Mesgei´. Sorry. So sorry. So mesgei´."

This sobbing of hers got her sister sobbing along with her. And this got me going even worse than I ever believed I could. Even Matuwes laid her own face down and I could see her shoulders hitching. I didn't dare look at Mak. And especially, I didn't want to watch while he wrapped my husband in skins.

"Agada," he said. "Help me get him onto the travois. Please."

I felt Agada shift behind me and I felt her move around me toward Falcon.

I heard the shifting of skins and blankets.

I heard the sigh of weight going onto the travois.

I felt Mak move to my side.

I heard him whisper into my ear, "It's done. He's wrapped. He's ready to go. It's time to leave. We must go. Now."

***

Mak wouldn't let me take a turn pulling the travois with Falcon's body on it. When I tried to take over from Matuwes, to give her a rest, he pulled my hands away from the poles.

"It's not far. We have plenty of help to do this." His eyes turning behind me reminded me that two of Second Son's Spirit Questers were still with us, their eyes full of held-back tears. "You must rest, Keskoua. You will need your strength for the days to come."

"I'm not gesnugwai, I'm not sick." I pushed his arm off my shoulder, not because I didn't like the feel of it. Because I did. I wanted to be inside his arms again. I wanted to be inside anyone's arms again, but especially his. I thought that might keep me from crying.

"Let the Spirit Questers take a turn," Matuwes said. "They need to learn our ways."

"Those little boys?" I snapped at her. "Look at them. They are devastated with the loss of Falcon. They looked up to him. I would not force that on anyone, especially a child."

Agada spoke. "It's much easier to recognize pain in someone else than in ourselves. But once we recognize it in someone else, it's easier to see it in ourselves if we turn around and look. E´e? Second Son told me that, too."

Matuwes paused to let one of the Spirit Questers take the travois from her. I could tell by the way his shoulders and head changed that he did so with pride.

I turned to Agada. "E´e. You are right. It seems you will make a wise healer. I'm sorry. I should do what I'm told and not make any decisions. E´e?"

"E´e."

"For now, at least." I reached for the poles again but both Mak and Agada pulled me away.

"Let it be," she said. "The boys need to have experiences. Please allow them to participate in the sacred ceremony. This is part of it, is it not?"

I let myself step away. An arm went around me. It was Solange's. It felt good.

"How are you doing?" I asked her. "Are you managing all this?"

"Better than you, it looks like. I've heard you like to argue, but—"

"That was a serious question, Solange. You loved him, too."

"Everybody did. And I told you, I did not love him in that way. Stop projecting."

This made me laugh. "App? Projecting?"

"Yes. Projecting. Or are you simply wanting to have a philosophical discussion about something?"

"Who are you?" I smiled at her. These two girls were beginning to make me doubt myself, my ability to read people.

"No less than Matuwes. She's not the only one who has had to hide her real self from people in order to stay alive."

"I would like to speak to you more about this some ti—"

Just then, Little Gracie came running around the corner of the path. "I heard you coming! You're back! You're all na... to´q..." Her eyes went to the form on the travois. "Oh."

Mak went to her and crouched down in front of her. "We are na to´q, yes. But not Falcon."

Little Gracie's hand went to her open mouth and she turned and ran back to where she had come from. "Mama. Charles. Mama. He's dead. He's dead. Falcon is dead."

Twenty-five

I remember most of what I did right after we arrived at Mak's temporary village. I had tea, the rest of our group ate something. I tried to eat but nothing wanted to go into my mouth. Not even a sweet.

Then after everyone had eaten, I did nothing but lie on skins and blankets in Mak's wikuom while the others prepared a Sacred Fire. They would be passing the Talking Stick and speaking of my husband. My dead husband. I would be able to hear everything, but I didn't know everyone's name to know who would be speaking. I knew some of them. Most? No. Not most. This was not my village. I didn't want to listen. I wanted only to sleep but knew I wouldn't be able to. I didn't want to. The voices would keep me awake and listening. Mak wanted me awake and listening. I wanted to be awake and listening. But at the same time, I didn't.

Mak had led me into his wikuom and had helped me lie down on the few blankets and skins that covered a very thin layer of cedars.

I turned my back to him.

"Try to rest. You'll need your strength. You'll be leaving early this evening with Falcon."

This was exactly what I didn't want to think about. Not until I had to. The closer we got to our own village, the truer it would be that my Falcon was gone.

"Everything will be ready. And I don't mean your physical strength.

You'll have help, of course. And it's only to Flower Stalk's village for this next step. One step at a time. Right? I'd be willing to bet you tell everyone that. Yes?"

I started to ask Mak who would be helping me but he put his fingers against my lips.

"Bear, J-B and Pierre will be taking over from there. Don't worry about anything from here to there, though. I'm sending the Spirit Questers with you and they'll—"

"All of them?"

"Three. The three from your village. They'll be going with you all the way to Port Royal. Then everyone will come back to help with the dikes. Don't worry about anything, Keskoua. Right now, you need your rest."

"But I—"

Again, Mak's fingers went to my lips. "Rest and listen."

I didn't want to listen. I didn't want to listen to Mak. I didn't want to listen to what the people around the Sacred Fire would be saying about Falcon. I didn't want to listen to my own self. I distracted myself by caressing the blankets and cedars I was lying on.

"You are Lnu Saqamaw," I said. "Why do you sleep on such meager bedding?"

"It is *because* I am Chief that I end up with meager bedding. Someone comes to me for help, what else can I do but help them? That's what Chiefs do, do they not?"

"Does anyone else know of this?" I rolled onto my back. At least there were no stones under me.

The corner of Mak's mouth went up.

"What's so funny?"

"If I were asking you that question, would you not assume I was trying to discover how many lovers you have had?"

I must have looked at him strangely because his laugh came fully out.

"Never mind. Lie still. Let me cover you." He tucked the blankets and skins around me.

It felt good. "Wela'lin."

"You're more than welcome, Keskoua. Sleep if you wish, but we will be sitting close enough to my wikuom for you to hear us around the Sacred Fire. But far enough from my wikuom so it does not go up in flames with you in it."

"You would put that into my head, wouldn't you, Mak?" I did not smile. I wanted to but I didn't. This made me very proud of myself. "Is this your way of making sure I don't fall asleep? That I will listen to everything in case *you* fall asleep during the Sacred Fire? When you are supposed to be listening to every single little complaint everybody will no doubt be making?"

He adjusted the blanket under my chin and patted my cheek. "I will be back after the Sacred Fire is safely out. I need a rest, too. A quick sleep to refresh myself before more of the day's activities demand my attention. And there will be more."

"Have you had any sleep in the last two days?"

"As you can see, I have nowhere to lie down—or even sit down—other than where you are lying. We will have to share. Do you have a problem with that?"

I didn't. I would need someone's arms around me in case a melgwisgat, un cauchemar, a nightmare, decided to visit me if I happened to fall asleep. Mak's arms around me would help me in another way: being that close to him, to a man, any man other than Falcon, would keep me awake, aware and watching. Tqoqwejg, wild cats, were not the only creatures who could sneak up on you without your noticing.

A man's voice from outside Mak's wikuom. "Maintenant là. Lnu Saqamaw. Le feu. Ça va."

"I'll be right there, Charles." To me, he said, "That's Charles. Afia's husband. He is a good man. A wise one. He's been instrumental in the rebuilding of the dikes. He seems to have an eye for that sort of thing.

We were in business together."

"Business?"

"Mak! The fire. It's going."

"I'll be right there." Mak bent down and kissed my forehead. "I will see you later. Listen to everything they say. You and I will need to make plans based on what is discussed."

"App?"

But he was gone with the answer in his head only.

I was beginning to notice that he didn't always answer my questions.

***

The Talking Stick went around the entire circle quickly with even Little Gracie saying kind things about Falcon. What else could anyone say about Falcon? He had been a good, kind man.

Then, Agada was the first to speak of other things. "This is going to send Second Son somewhere we don't want him to go."

A rumbling agreement went around the circle, but I heard no words.

Then Mak said, "Excuse me, Agada. Little Bat. You were successful?"

It seemed that Little Bat had returned.

"I was, Lnu Saqamaw. May I join the Sacred Fire?"

"Go check on Keskoua, please. She's in my wikuom."

Little Bat stepped inside Mak's wikuom. "Everything is na to´q, Keskoua?"

"E´e. You were able to find him?"

He stepped close to me and pulled the blanket up under my chin like Mak had done. And like my giju´, my mother, used to do to me, and like I did to my own children. "Yes. And Captain sends his gratitude to you."

"There's no need to treat me like a baby. And he should be thanking Agada. She's the one who gave us the information."

"You don't like it when I do that?"

"What? Give me credit for something I didn't do? Of course not."

Little Bat laughed. "I mean treat you like a baby."

"I like that less."

Little Bat stood up straight then and with a smile, said, "It's true what they say about you."

"What's that?"

"You aren't very good at lying."

Before I could respond, he was laughing and out of Mak's wikuom.

Agada was speaking. "… admired Falcon greatly. Depended on him for everything. He won't do well hearing this news."

"Well then, you'd best keep your voice down, girl." I did not recognize this voice, but I knew it was an elderly woman's voice and it was deep and scratchy, as though she had spent her life screaming at other people. But it might have been from the smoke.

"Why is that?"

"He's sleeping right over there. Among the trees."

Another woman's voice, this one's throat squeaking high, like a hawk's, with each intake of breath before she spoke, her voice barely hearable, said, "Passed out, more likely."

I heard a shuffle of clothing and Agada's voice from a different angle. Had she stood up?

"Sit down, Agada." Mak's voice.

Another shuffle of clothing and Agada's voice from where it had been. "What's wrong with him?"

Hawk Throat replied, "What else? Drunk."

"He was supposed to be helping replace the dikes but they sent him away," said Scratchy Voice. "He's of no use to anyone. As you should know. Then again, of what use are you to anyone with that disease of yours."

Solange spoke. "She has no disease. I am the one with the disease. Stop being so mean to everyone or I will spit on you and give it to you, too."

I heard one gasp, one hawk scream.

"May I speak?" This was Matuwes.

"Yes. Here." I knew that Agada had handed the Talking Stick to Matuwes.

Mak spoke. "Little Bat. Stay with Keskoua. Stand at the entrance so you can watch her and also convey any important information that she might miss." Then he whispered something I did not hear.

Little Bat appeared just outside the entrance and smiled at me.

I sat up, crossed my legs and reached for my cup of tea. I took a sip. It was cold but I didn't care. I listened.

"I am no healer."

I heard the scream of air going into Hawk Throat before she said, "You can say that again."

"Everything I learned, I learned from the people who took me away. That our medicines are from the Devil and should not ever be used."

"That's stupid," Little Bat whispered to me.

"Hush. Listen."

"They don't use medicines at all. They say all medicines are from the Devil. The Devil gives you the disease and if God wills it, God takes the disease away. No need for medicines. They are from the Devil. Hearing this for so many years and through so many beatings, I can't seem to get the right things into my head because of the fear of them. Something inside resists the information." She paused.

Little Bat made the motion for me that Matuwes was sipping something.

"I do, however, understand how people think and feel. That is something that never left me."

The laughter that came through the wall of Mak's wikuom was, I knew, from Scratchy Voice and Hawk Throat.

Mak spoke. "Show some respect for this woman. She has endured much."

"As though we haven't!" growled Scratchy Voice. "The woman beside me here can barely breathe because of the fires those English bastards have set everywhere. The smoke is killing people and Matuwes couldn't— now it sounds more like wouldn't—do a thing about it. We had to send word to Port Royal, for the love of Christ, to get someone who knows something, to come help us."

Little Bat pointed at me and smiled wide.

"Have some respect for this woman."

The following grumble was demonstrated by Little Bat who folded his arms and made the corners of his mouth turn down.

I silenced a laugh with my hand.

Matuwes continued. "Agada has spent time with our visiting healer, Keskoua. Our young Agada has learned a great deal from her. But I think Agada knew a great deal even before that. I recommend you allow her to learn, to become your new healer."

Sounds of surprise—with no grumbles—floated through the wikuom wall.

I rose to my feet and went to stand beside Little Bat from where I could watch without being easily seen by everyone.

Mak was on the left side of the circle. His eyes flicked to mine. There were several people, mostly our people, sitting cross-legged in the circle. There were also several of our people, mostly men, standing, legs wide, arms crossed, near the trees on the other side of the circle. I knew that many of the Acadian men had been killed in the attacks. The ones who remained were working hard on getting the dikes replaced so were absent. Our people helped with the dikes, too, yes, of course they did. But I think the message had gone out that there would be important things to discuss at this Sacred Fire so they had decided to come. The death of Falcon was only one of the reasons.

Matuwes, who was seated on the other side of Mak, continued. "I am not a healer. I admit that. But I am not unintelligent. Pretending I was a healer was my way of trying to keep all my bad memories hidden away from myself. Being a healer—I admit, a pretend one—made me feel good. Strong. Of value. It made me take my mind off everything that was trying to come out with all this… this terror going on and… but mostly, reminding me of other bad times. I know that now. Fear is fear. One fear threatens to bring up a forgotten one. It's like having a wasp nest in your head. You don't dare disturb anything."

I knew she had seen me, but she still leaned back to point her voice at the wikuom's wall as if I were still inside. "Keskoua. If you are hearing me. I will show you where I hid the things from your munti. I didn't use them all. I lied about that."

I saw Agada's eyes get wide and she glanced over at Little Bat. I know she saw me then, too, but she also pretended she hadn't. She was seated beside Matuwes.

"I have heard that going to new places can help make us feel better even though new things can make us afraid," said Matuwes. "The same with experiencing new people. Can we trust this new person? Or going to new lands where there are new rules of living and where, if we make a mistake, they might hurt us. Or worse. The fear of doing these new things hides the fears already hidden away inside us. It makes us not think of them because we pile these new fears on top of the old ones. We can bury them. *Try* to bury them. It doesn't make them go away, though. It just makes it harder to find them if we need to know why we are angry or sad all the time." Her eyes went down to the Talking Stick in her hand. "Even if we understand the things on top of the pile and why they make us angry or sad…" She looked up again. "Like what the Maudits anglaises are doing to us now and have done to us before, those other things do *not* fall out of us. They stay there. Keskoua told me these buried things can make us sick. Or make us think only of our own selves and not about anybody else. Which can make others sick. We must not do that. Not ever. I must not. Ever again."

"I understand what you are saying," interrupted a tiny little woman full of wrinkled skin. It was Scratchy Voice. She would be perhaps seventy, or even eighty, winters old. She was one of our people and sat on the far side of the circle. "And I'm not even angry with you, Matuwes, for telling me something I should already know." She tipped her head to one side and her eyes went up to the sky. Her small smile told me she was ashamed. "It *was* something I already knew. But forgot. What you say is true. Of course, it's true. And we should always remember this." She looked at the others around the circle before her eyes went to a younger woman, an Acadian, on my side of her, one who was taking deep breaths through her mouth. I guessed this would be Hawk Throat. "But how? It's not easy to face everything that's going on and not want to crawl into our own cave of anger and sadness—and especially fear, yes—where we have only our own selves, or those closest to us..." She smiled at the younger woman, then leaned over to let me see more of herself past the turn of Mak's wikuom. To me, she said, "This is my son's wife." Then to Matuwes, "Should I not care for her more than for others? I don't think that's being selfish."

Around the circle and behind it from those standing, heads bowed and voices murmured in respectful agreement with Scratchy Voice.

Matuwes spoke. "I have learned a lot. About this woman. And from this woman." She put the Talking Stick into her left hand and her right hand went upside down with the fingers toward Agada. "I wish to recommend her as our new healer. There is an opening, after all. Is there not?"

Around the circle, everyone nodded and said "E´e," even Agada. Those standing behind them said, "E´e," too.

"I accept," said Agada. "It is a great honor you bestow on me. But I have much to learn."

"Don't we all have much to learn," said Scratchy Voice. She turned toward Matuwes. "Mesgei´, I'm sorry."

A hawk scream and the younger woman coughed out, "Me too." She screamed in another breath before she spoke. "Agada. Can you heal my throat? I think it was burned in the fire that brought our cabin to the ground."

Agada's eyes met those of Hawk Throat and she nodded at her. "I will try my best."

"And my husband and my children have nowhere to live. Nor have I."

Mak's eyes met those of Hawk Throat now. "We are building new wikuoms for just that purpose. Two are completed, thanks to Charles and Afia. You may choose."

Hawk Throat's shoulders went down to where they were supposed to be, but her breathing did not improve.

My shoulders went up. "I thought you told me there weren't any vacant—"

Giggles erupted from Solange and Agada and elsewhere in the circle. I couldn't see who else because my eyes were trying to set Mak on fire.

To me, Mak said, "Wait your turn." Then to Agada, "I know you were wishing to speak, Agada, but I wish to say something. May I have the Talking Stick, Matuwes?"

He took it from her, glanced over at me and said, "Stop that."

More giggles.

"There is but one ship left in the harbor and no one has seen patrol boats for two days."

The man sitting between Agada and Little Gracie nodded his head at Mak. Afia was on the other side of Little Gracie. I was certain, then, that this man would be Charles, the husband of Afia.

Mak said, "Thank you for keeping track of this, Charles. You do so many things for all of us."

"I had help, Chief," said Charles, indicating one of Second Son's Spirit Questers across from him. The boy had his back to me. "He's a smart young man."

Mak turned his attention to the others again. "I think this means they are no longer watching us like they were. Which is peculiar, but I think it means that we can now move through the bush at any time, not just at low tide. But with caution."

Mutters of happiness and relief went around the circle and from the men behind it.

"Has anyone seen any of them in the bush lately?"

Mutters of moqwa´, no, went around the circle and from the men behind it.

One of the men near the trees said, "Only the one," and he pointed toward Agada.

"We must still maintain diligence. These men will stop at nothing to destroy French control over Acadia." Mak turned toward Agada. "Has your friend… Hammy, is it?"

She nodded.

"Has this Hammy provided any information about why things are now so quiet on board that ship?"

She shook her head.

"That's settled until we get more information then. But keep a watchful eye, everyone. And let us know if you see or hear anything amiss. Anything, no matter how insignificant it might seem at the time."

Nods and mutters of agreement went around again.

"You will let us know, Agada? If you hear anything from this Hammy person?"

Agada nodded her head.

"Now I have more surprises." Mak's eyes went to me first, then around the circle to the others, all around. "Some, you may not agree with."

A hawk scream, then, "Oh?"

"I will be leaving this community. I will no longer be Chief."

Afia, Little Gracie and Charles were the only ones who didn't gasp.

Even I gasped.

"Where's he going to?" Little Bat asked me.

"Hush."

"I will be asking Keskoua to be my woman, my wife—"

"*APP?*"

At the sound of my voice, everyone turned now to look at me.

The sound from Hawk Throat made my eyes squeeze together. Then, "You can't get married! They burned all the churches!"

Scratchy Voice croaked. "When is this supposed to happen?"

"Yes, Mak," I said, stepping away from the entrance of the wikuom. "When is this supposed to happen? And do you not think that I should be included in this decision?"

"You were right," whispered Solange across Mak to Agada, loudly enough for everyone to hear. "She does have a temper."

Laughter rippled around the circle and behind it.

"It's not funny. Explain to me, Mak. What are you saying?"

"I will be moving to Port Royal. I will be setting up an inn there. My sister, Afia, and her husband, Charles, and Little Gracie…"

Little Gracie smiled over at me and wiggled her fingers.

"… will be continuing to repair the inn here. They are almost done. It will be theirs entirely. Mine in Port Royal will be mine entirely. Oh. And it will be yours, too, of course. But I know you have your own important work so I won't be asking you to help out or do any work for me."

"And I'm supposed to… What? Thank you or something? The answer is no. Absolutely and completely and entirely and forever, no."

"So much for that idea," laughed Charles. "And funny how a talking circle's discipline of one person at a time can fall apart when certain subjects arise."

Laughter went around the circle and behind it again.

As I returned to the blankets and skins in Mak's wikuom—with Little

Bat following to the entrance—there was no laughter from me. That was for certain. There was nothing the least bit amusing about Mak's announcement.

Just as my head hit my munti pillow, I heard Second Son's voice demand. "Who is wrapped up in skins on the travois?"

"Oh, no. Who woke him?" Agada's voice asked in a loud whisper.

Little Bat struggled to hold in a laugh. "Looks like Waddling Duck has come out of his fog nest."

"App?"

"He waddles when he's drunk. We don't call him that in front of him, or his boys, of course."

"That's not very nice, Little Bat. He's…" And here I paused to think of something nice to say about Second Son. But I couldn't think of anything.

To try to stop us both from laughing, I was up and standing beside the entrance to the wikuom again. Little Bat shuffled to stand in front of me but to the side, to protect, yet allow me to watch.

The other Spirit Quester was with him. He answered. "I did. I woke him up. What of it? He was lying there silent and unmoving. I was concerned. He would have done the same for me."

"I do not doubt that," Agada answered. "But have you no idea what he is like when awakened from—"

"I said, who is wrapped up in skins on the travois?"

Mak rose to his feet.

"Come with me, Second Son. We have complications to discuss." To the others, he said, "Matuwes will continue in my absence."

"App? What complications? I demand to know who is on the travois."

Mak did not, I noticed, take Second Son by the arm or in any way attempt to touch him, but instead, he walked toward the bush where Second Son had come from. "Come along. We must make sure your Spirit Quester there did not leave anything the enemy can find."

The Spirit Quester opened his mouth to say something but Matuwes stopped him with, "The Sacred Fire is over. Help me get to my feet, young man."

Second Son took a step to follow Mak. He paused. He turned back to look at the travois once again, then followed Mak into the bush.

Twenty-six

Matuwes, Agada, and Solange began chattering away around me like a group of titiesg, blue jays, around an injured mouse.

"What is he talking about?" asked Matuwes. "Setting up an inn in Port Royal? Marrying *you*?"

"I don't think I'm a chenoo or anything, Matuwes," I said, remembering what Matuwes had been talking about, hiding feelings under feelings in the hopes they would go away.

"And with Falcon lying right over there?" Matuwes pointed.

I didn't need to be reminded where my husband's body lay.

"What will happen with the community if Mak leaves?" asked Agada.

"Matuwes would become Lnu Saqamaw," I said.

"What's that you say?" Scratchy Voice pushed her way into our group. "Matuwes as Chief? Are you out of your mind?"

"I'll vote for Matuwes as Chief," said Charles.

"I will also," said Afia.

"Me too," Little Gracie added.

Rumbles of e´e went through the rest of the people who were there.

One of the men near the trees said, "We all agree here." As they moved off, he added, in English, "Back to the damned dikes."

"Sure you don't mean *dammed* dikes?" laughed another man. "Isn't that what they are supposed to be? Dams?"

163

"That's what I meant. That's why I used English. Those bâtards are good for something then, e´e?"

They laughed as they disappeared into the trees.

"It's not my community." I made my shoulders go up. "But I would agree, too, that Matuwes would make an excellent Chief."

"I've never heard of anything so ridiculous," said Scratchy Voice.

"*Undskyld mig. Hej.*" Agada made me think of a snapping turtle. "Excuse me. Hello. There's no need for rudeness."

We settled down again.

"I asked you, what will happen if Mak leaves?"

A hawk scream, then "Chaos. That's what will happen."

"I agree," said Scratchy Throat. "For one thing, Matuwes is female."

Afia pushed in between Scratchy Voice and Agada. "And? By that you are saying what?"

Hawk Throat screamed and a giggle came out. "Much as I respect you, Belle-Mère, Mother-in-Law, Afia is right. What's that got to do with anything?" She paused for a squealing breath. "I meant that chaos always follows change. The more important the change, the greater the chaos."

"She was away for many years. She is no longer one of us. And those years… and she even admitted it… you heard her… those years made her become a…" Scratchy Voice paused. "She became… Well, she admitted it. Just now. She admitted that she's… I don't trust her. She can be cruel. And she lies. Right?"

No one said a word. We all had our eyes on the face of Scratchy Voice, waiting for her to finish what she had to say.

"Shall I get you a shovel?" asked Matuwes and I couldn't believe she was actually smiling. "So you can keep digging that hole for yourself?"

"Oh, stop it." Scratchy Voice grabbed Hawk Throat roughly by the arm and tried to pull her away. "I do not agree. Let's go."

A scream and a "No. I want to hear what Matuwes's plans are." Scream. "She is now our Chief. Or will be as soon as Mak leaves."

A huff from Scratchy Voice and off she stomped like a male spruce grouse showing his behind to a reluctant hen.

"I don't have any plans," said Matuwes, her smile replaced by a frown of worry. "I need to talk to Mak. I need to talk to all of you. No, I need to listen to all of you. I—"

Mak stepped out of the trees just as Scratchy Voice went stomping past him.

"What's wrong with her?"

A scream, "She doesn't adjust well to change."

"Where's Second Son?" I asked.

"I told him about Falcon. He's upset. Of course. He went into the bush. Said he was going to relieve himself, but he needs to be taken care of, watched." Mak turned to where Second Son's two Spirit Questers were huddled close together talking. "You there. Go look after him."

"Look after who?"

"Second Son. Who else? Do you know where he has his whiskey hidden?"

Both boys laughed. The taller one said, "Where does he not have whiskey hidden?"

"Go look after him. And bring back some whiskey."

Looking like hungry baby robins, the boys looked at each other.

"Don't ask questions. Just do it. Three bottles should be enough."

They looked at each other again then rushed away into the trees.

***

"Whiskey," I said.

"He says he's going to stop drinking but he knows he can't do it all at once. He wants to wait until you get Falcon back to your village." Mak paused. "He says you can help him go through what he has to go through."

"I can try but it's really up to him."

"And right now, we need to vote on having Matuwes take over from me as Chief."

Agada said, "Pretty much everyone else has agreed that it's a good idea. I think so, from what I have learned about her."

"I have heard her talking with Mak," said Solange. "And she has given him good ideas. That's why I voted yes."

"I know Mak's my brother so you might think I am showing favoritism, but I agree with his choice," said Afia.

"Matuwes is always nice to me," said Little Gracie. "She has some good ideas about stuff. That's why I said yes."

Charles added, "She was very close to Chief Apistanewj." He turned to me to say, "He was killed. He was our Chief." Then he looked around at the others again. "She knows all of us here. That's why I would choose her. The only one we haven't heard from is you, Mak."

"Perhaps ask the question another way?" offered Matuwes. "Ask who does not want me to be Chief here."

No one spoke.

I said, "The woman who left said no."

"That's one of many," said Charles.

"I agree," said Mak. "Of course, I do. It was my idea in the first place, was it not?"

"It should be everyone," insisted Matuwes. "Everyone should agree."

A scream, "Just because she doesn't like or trust you, doesn't mean she wouldn't want you as Chief." A scream. "I'll go ask her." Hawk Throat rushed away.

From the other side of us, from the path, came voices. Familiar voices.

Bear appeared first. He was followed by J-B, Pierre, then Flower Stalk.

"That's it for bodies," said Flower Stalk with a smile and a face full of relief. "We have none with us this time. We are here to find out how we should handle the dikes at our end."

"Wonderful." Mak hugged her, then Pierre, then J-B and Bear. "We have just been making changes here." He stretched his arm out toward Matuwes. "Meet our new Chief."

"We have not finished voting," she said.

"Her?" said J-B, throwing a glance at me.

"Yes. Her," I told him, trying to send a message with my eyes that everything was na to´q.

I think it worked because he shrugged but he made a face at the same time.

"Well, Matuwes?" said Mak. "Are you ready to make suggestions as to how they can help with the dikes?"

"Will you be helping at our end, too, Keskoua?" asked Bear. "At Flower Stalk's village? They've decided to call it a village. Might as well. Nobody else lives anywhere else near her. As a group, at least."

Before I could speak, Mak had taken Bear's arm and was leading him toward the travois with Falcon on it. I did not hear what words were exchanged between them, but Bear's quick glance back at me said he understood there would be no helping with the dikes for him, J-B, Pierre or me just yet.

He returned to the group. "We must leave immediately."

"Why? What's going on?" asked Flower Stalk.

"The travois."

"Yes?"

"It holds Falcon."

"Ah."

"We have had a small ceremony here but he must go back to your village," Mak said. "As soon as possible. To be buried."

"I'm well aware of our traditions," snapped Bear. Then kindly to me, "Are you na to´q, Keskoua?"

"What do you think? She's as na to´q as she can be," said Mak without a smile or anything else on his face. "Of course she is not na to´q. I will stay here for a few more days to help with the transition of my responsibilities into the hands of Matuwes, but I will follow as soon as possible."

"App? Why?" Bear's eyes made him look like his head was hurting him.

"And in the meantime, J-B," continued Mak. "I expect you will take care of her for me."

I responded to J-B's frown at me with a shrug.

Bear said, "What's going on here? You are planning something?"

"Yes," said Agada. "He is going to be moving to your village."

I've never seen such a strange look on the face of anyone, especially never on Bear's face.

Puffed up as tall as he could be, Bear stepped toward Mak. Mak did not flinch. "What brought this on?" Then Bear's eyes pierced into mine so fiercely, mine turned away.

"Hé, hé, vous deux. Assez!" Charles stepped between them. "That's enough, you two."

Just as all three men began to push each other, Scratchy Voice came rushing in with a baby in her arms. She was followed by a young woman, very much out of breath. Hawk Throat followed.

"Keskoua. Agada. Please. The baby needs help. It can't breathe right."

***

Both Agada and I rushed toward Scratchy Voice to see what was happening with the baby.

Behind me, several things were happening all at once. Bear was insisting everyone leave with Falcon's travois, including me, immediately. Hawk Throat was telling Mak that Scratchy Voice had agreed to vote for Matuwes. J-B was arguing with Pierre about not staying with Flower Stalk. That Pierre should be coming back to the fort with the group or he would be facing a firing squad for desertion. That he could always return later, when he got permission from Gabbie. That it would be easy for him to get permission because Gabbie was his uncle. Pierre was not wanting to agree. Pierre did not want to be separated from Flower Stalk for even the briefest of times. Matuwes was spouting ideas to Flower Stalk while asking

Charles—who was beside me and Agada—his opinion, too, about how best to set up the remaining dikes. And Little Gracie was complaining about a funny smell coming from the skins on the travois.

"Do you know anything about how to help improve this baby's condition?" I asked Agada.

"First of all, water. We need to keep him... What's the word?"

"I don't think there is a word. He just needs good water inside him that will help to flush out the bad water from his lungs. Like a fast stream carries everything along with it."

"Ah. Yes. Thank you. I'd say the baby is perhaps a year old so he could drink water from a cup?"

"He just passed eleven moons," said the baby's mother. "And yes, he's been drinking from a cup for a while now." Any pride she might have shown us was overshadowed by the fear on her face. Her whole body showed signs of fear. "Also, he still drinks from me." She touched her breast. She coughed.

Agada continued. "He needs warmth. Rest. What else? I'm so nervous I am forgetting."

"Steam," I said. "Don't forget steam."

"Does anyone have a pot?" she called out. "With water in it? Hurry."

From the side of my eye, I saw Little Bat run off into the trees. He returned almost instantly with a fire-blackened cooking pot. "Where's the water?"

"Over here," said Little Gracie. "They put it over here for today." She led him away.

I heard Matuwes suggest that Flower Stalk and Charles work from both sides of the line of dikes to close in, but to put some up here and there along the line so the edge lines converging might not be as easily noticed. "When they are sprinkled around," she said, "they are not as easily seen and also, it's easier to quickly fill in the spots without being noticed as much."

"Bring the baby into this wikuom," I said, indicating Mak's wikuom. I took the baby from Scratchy Voice.

"Hey," Mak said, protesting. "There are other wikuoms."

"I see why Mak chose you to be Chief," said Flower Stalk. "When he first said it, I…"

"Never mind that now. What do you think of my idea? Yes? Or no?" She called out. "Charles?"

"Yes," said Charles.

"Yes," said Flower Stalk. "I agree with that idea, too."

"Agada," Matuwes called out. "Do you know where they hid the wheat seeds?"

"I think where they make the whiskey," she replied. Then she leaned down to hold her listening device to the baby's chest. "It's not as bad as I thought. It sounds worse on the outside of him." She smiled over at the baby's mother then up at me, then down at the baby.

Agada took the baby from me then, and brought him into Mak's wikuom where Charles was already setting up rocks to set the pot over what would be a small fire.

Behind us, Little Bat held the pot that was obviously full of water because his muscles were bulging out.

"This is heavy."

"Maybe we don't need as much water in that," I said. "It will get boiling faster?"

A scream. "Oh. You already found a pot." Hawk Throat held a second pot, this one not as fire blackened as the other.

"We can use both," said Agada. "Little Bat? Pour some of that water into the other pot."

Little Bat did.

I ran out of the wikuom with one of the small sticks that Charles had collected, to touch it to the remaining coals of the Sacred Fire to start it burning.

"Keskoua." This was Bear's voice. "We are ready to leave. Let's go."

"Go ahead. I'll catch up."

"You are not traveling alone!" both Bear and Mak said this at the same time. I could only imagine what their faces looked like. I didn't bother looking. I was busy. And I didn't want to know anyway.

"You aren't going anywhere with Falcon without me." Second Son appeared from the trees to my right.

Beside him, one of the young Spirit Questers stood holding a sack with bottles poking at its insides like a baby's foot in its mother's belly.

"Merde," said J-B.

"Hurry it up, then," said Bear. "And Keskoua. You are coming, too."

"Do you still need me?" asked Little Bat. "I should go with J-B."

"Everything's ready in here," said Charles from inside the wikuom. "We just need to start the fire."

"Go. Go," I said to Little Bat. "Thank you, Charles. And no, I'm not going with you, Bear. I have to help Agada with this baby."

"We can't wait for you," Bear said.

"We'll wait for you at Flower Stalk's village," said Pierre.

"No we won't," Bear growled. "We have to get Falcon back. He must be buried. Soon. He should have been buried already. Keskoua! Come! Now!"

"No!"

Between Agada and me, we got the baby settled in the wikuom and Charles had steam coming out of the pot in no time at all.

I heard Flower Stalk promise Matuwes that she would be back and forth to further plan the rebuilding of the dikes. "And I'm sorry I was mean to you."

"I don't blame you," I heard Matuwes laugh. "I would have done the same to me."

Then Bear's voice: "Last chance, Keskoua."

"No."

Twenty-seven

I wasn't surprised that Mak was angry with me when I left to go to Flower Stalk's village and that I planned to go alone.

"No one can be spared," I told him. "They need all the hands they can get to help rebuild the dikes. And Agada needs people to help her, too."

"Are you absolutely certain?" asked Matuwes. "I can find someone to go with you."

"It's not far. I'll be fine."

Mak reluctantly agreed and told me to be careful. I expected him to kiss my forehead again but as I leaned in to accept it, he pushed up my chin with his fingers and touched my lips with his. They were so soft, I felt a weakness wash over me and through my entire body.

***

He was right and Bear had been right.

I hadn't gone far before I knew I was being followed. At first, I thought Mak had decided to keep watch over me either himself or by sending someone along behind me after I left. I had a knife in my munti, another in my leg wrappings, and one in my belt, but I didn't think it was an animal. I didn't know of any animal that would follow a person the way someone was following me. Not if the animal was looking for something to eat, that is.

Then up ahead, I heard a branch snap on one side then on the other side. A branch snapped behind me, too. Then I heard a rush of leaves and branches as three men stepped out to surround me. They all wore jackets over vests with buttons everywhere. They were Maudits anglaises.

"Do… you… speak… English?" asked the shortest one, stepping around from behind me.

"I… do… and… quite… well… thank… you."

The man frowned as he glanced over at one of his companions, the only one wearing a hat.

The man with the hat said nothing. His face told me nothing either.

The short man said, "We… can… continue… to… speak… very… slowly… if… you… wish."

"*Por que você gostaria de perder todo o nosso tempo fazendo isso? Pourquoi voudriez-vous perdre tout notre temps à le faire? Waarom zou je al onze tijd daarmee verspillen?*"

This time it was the man with the hat who glanced over at the short one. "What is she…? That last bit was Dutch, wasn't it?"

I could tell that the third man, who stood slightly behind the man with the hat, was doing his best to control his smile but I could see it in his eyes. "It was. It was also Portuguese and French. I think we'd better keep a close eye on this one."

"Well?" said the short man. "What did she say?"

"She said, 'Why would you want to waste all of our time doing that?'"

"Well I'll be damned," said the short man. "I didn't realize these creatures were that intelligent. So she speaks, what, three languages then? Portuguese, French and Dutch?"

In English, I said, "Plus my own language and, of course, I… speak… English… too."

The short man turned to the third man. "But, Zeke. She… She appears to be mocking us. Is she?" He twirled on me and took a step toward me. "Are you mocking us?"

I shook my head. "Just you."

The laugh finally escaped from the man called Zeke.

The man with the hat said, "My dear friend. How many times have I told you to have some respect for these people?"

The short man grumbled something as he turned away from me indicating we should follow him.

"I'm very sorry," Zeke said to me. "But you'll have to come with us. We really have nothing against you people, but since you all seem to be in cahoots with the Catholics, we need to see if we can find out anything of value whenever we run across one of you."

"Really. How interesting."

The short man turned to me. "Yes it is. It— Wait a minute. Obadiah, is she being sarcastic?"

The man with the hat, Obadiah, who had his hand on my elbow, said, "Jesus Christ, I swear to God you have to be one of the most unintelligent men I've ever known. Of course she's being sarcastic."

"How the hell am I supposed to know what goes on in the minds of these christly devils?"

I couldn't help myself. "A christly devil. I would say that would be… What's the word I'm thinking of? Ah, yes. That would be something of a phenomenon, wouldn't it?"

Zeke said, "I'm starting to like this one. I hope we don't have to burn her at the stake."

"If they ask for my vote, I'll insist we do," said Obadiah.

"Come on. I know very well you're against that practice."

"True enough. Now I only hope we haven't cursed ourselves by joking about it. You know how the Devil works."

"Why are you so against them?" I asked. "I've heard, and I've seen with my own two eyes—or, do I have three eyes? There are some people who have three eyes, you know. And those aren't Catholics. They're—"

"They're Hindu," interrupted Zeke. "They live in India. Do you know about that country?"

"Only what I've heard. And, of course, that you people named our people after the Indians in India." I was the only one who laughed. "How far wrong could anyone be?" But I got serious again quickly. I didn't think it would be a good idea to tease these men. Only the one called Zeke seemed to have a sense of humor. "I've never met a Hindu. Not that I know of." And here, my voice got much louder as I spoke directly to Obadiah, the man with the hat. "But I wouldn't set them on fire if I did."

"Only those possessed by the Devil will actually burn."

"You're saying, then, that every partridge or fish we accidentally overcook is actually possessed by this devil of yours? That it burns on its own? Baby lambs? Chipmunks and squirrels. Worms?"

Obadiah stopped walking but didn't turn. "That's ridiculous. The only animals possessed by the Devil are wolves and snakes. And perhaps spiders and mosquitoes. And yes, maybe worms."

I turned to Zeke. He wasn't laughing. He was nodding agreement.

"You people are scaring me, you know."

Obadiah began walking again. "And as we should be. It's for your own good, missy. Without fear, we would succumb entirely to the Devil's wishes."

"So to be certain, then, just burn everything?"

"Yes," blurted out the short man.

"Of course not," said Obadiah.

Zeke muttered, "Better to be sure sometimes." I couldn't tell if this man was joking or not right then.

Nor could I imagine living a life in constant fear of something invisible. We had our chenoo, but at least it could be reasoned with.

By the time we reached the waterline, where one of their ships was anchored far out in the bay, where the tide wouldn't ground it—Agada had been right, there was only one—I was almost believing in their devil.

But I had no doubt that it wasn't me or my people, or the Acadians, or chickens, wolves or mosquitoes who were in any way possessed by this devil of theirs. They were the ones possessed.

Under a single freshly chopped-off branch lay a boat with its nose pulled up on shore. It was about two times bigger than a whaling boat, so would have been able to take us four plus two times that.

"Now," said Zeke. "You can see that we have a boat here that can take all of us to the ship."

I looked over at it. "Yes. I see it. I smell it, too. If you were hunting on land with that thing, there would be no animals for miles around. You'd all starve."

Obadiah rubbed his sleeve under his nose. "It's not a pleasant odor, is it? You get used to it."

"No choice but to get used to it," said Zeke. "Without tar on boats' bottoms, we'd all sink."

"I wonder if it smells stronger to them than it does to us," muttered the short man. "**They are rather animal-like, aren't they?**"

My mouth opened but I knew this was not the time or place to let my thoughts escape. I had to control myself. I had no idea what these men were planning to do with me.

"We could take you to the ship. But I think it best if we question you right here. On land. In case we make a mess."

"Mess?" asked Obadiah.

"You know. Blood."

"Oh! No blood, please. I dislike the sight of it." The short man shivered.

"That's not funny," I said. "But wait. You're serious, aren't you?"

"I most certainly am."

I wasn't sure if the man called Zeke was still trying to make a joke or not. I wasn't sure, either, if I wanted to know. It was seeming to me, lately, that I wasn't wanting to know a lot of things. Was Matuwes right about me as well? Was I trying to hide some deep, dark secrets of my own? I had some. I knew that. And I also knew that Mak was triggering something I didn't want to remember. I remembered it, I just didn't *want* to. Falcon had been the only man who didn't frighten me when he got close.

"We'll sit here by the boat and talk."

The short man and the man called Obadiah, the man with the hat, lowered themselves onto boulders. Zeke pointed to the ground, indicating I should sit there.

I sat. I crossed my legs.

Zeke sat. He crossed his legs.

"What are you doing?" The short man yelled out at Zeke. "Only Devils sit with their legs crossed!"

"Oh," I said. "Does that mean he'll catch on fire soon? We savages like to discuss matters of importance around a fire. This is wonderful. You are such accommodating people."

"Is she—?"

"Yes, she is," said Zeke and Obadiah together.

"With that," said Obadiah, "I am going to keep watch to ensure that we have not been followed. "Carry on."

Obadiah got up off his rock and went away to where we had come from.

The short man got off his rock and crouched down beside Zeke.

Zeke pointed to the short man. "I'm Zeke. You may call him Nation."

"That's his name? Nation? It holds great promise. That he will some day rule."

"My full name is Damnation. There's only one place I will be able to rule with a name like that."

This man, Nation, wasn't acting like he thought this was funny. Not at all.

"Who would give their baby a name like that?"

"Puritans," said Zeke. "Us."

At the same time, Nation said, "Who else?"

Zeke wasn't smiling either. "His father is a church elder. Nation's mother was very beautiful."

"Was?"

"She died in childbirth."

"I see." I turned to Nation. "I'm guessing your father was upset and blamed his Devil for her death?"

"No. He blamed me."

"It was actually the congregation," Zeke put in, patting Nation's shoulder. "You did not kill your mother."

"He's right. Your father's the one who put you in there," I said. "And your mother let him. So it had nothing to do with you. You weren't around to ask." My attempt at trying to lighten the mood didn't work. It might have made it worse.

"My mother was beautiful so a witch. Evil."

At this, I laughed.

"See? She laughs at this. Proves she is one as well. With her magic spells and those cursed, evil objects she probably carries in that bag." Nation pointed at my munti.

This made me realize that I still had my munti with me. With its knife inside it. I had removed it from my shoulder but it rested on the ground by my right thigh. Why had they not taken it from me? They had not looked into my clothing to find my two knives concealed there, either. What kind of questioners were these men?

Zeke leaned forward with his elbow on one knee, ready to say something but Nation kept speaking.

"She calls them medicines, I would say. Just ask her. All medicines are the work of the Devil. You know that."

With his smile only in his eyes, Zeke asked, "Do you call them medicines?"

I laughed again. "What else should I call them?"

"Do not speak of them at all. The Lord God makes us ill because we deserve it and he cures us if we merit a cure." Nation turned again to Zeke. "I cannot believe these people."

"I suppose we are even in that case."

"Ask her what she means by *that*," Nation demanded.

Zeke turned to me with his mouth ready to ask but I spoke instead. "I can't believe you people, either, is what I meant by *that*."

"Enough talk," muttered Nation. "We are to extract information from this creature. I suggest we begin."

"Yes. Please do," I said. "The quicker we get this over with, the quicker I can be on my way again."

I didn't like the look that passed between Zeke and Nation.

"Right?"

Zeke began. "How do you know Edward Gooden?"

I don't know how, but I managed to keep my face from showing my surprise. I hoped so, anyway. "Who?"

The side of Zeke's mouth went up. "You may as well just tell us. We don't want to have to torture it out of you."

"Speak for yourself, Zeke."

"You're going to torture me?"

Nation pulled something out of one of his pockets. Even before he began unfolding them, I knew what they were: pigeon messages. I relaxed. Two of them were very white. I knew these were made of birchbark, so they had been sent by me. Those from Edward had a grayness to them. They were made of paper.

"Can you explain why Edward has been sending you messages? Messages exposing our plans for attack? How long has this been going on, pray tell?"

"May I see those?" I reached out my hand.

Like a child hiding something he didn't want his mother to see, Nation clutched the messages to his chest. "No. You most certainly may not touch these."

"How do I know you're telling the truth, then?"

"How dare you accuse me of lying."

"Take it easy, Nation. She's just trying to get you going." To me, Zeke said, "We know Edward well. We know he has been sending messages to you for many years. We know you two are friends. There's no problem with that. We merely wish to learn if you two have been exchanging information that should not be in enemy hands."

I laughed and pointed at Nation's closed hands. "They're in enemy hands right now."

"You are a funny and clever woman," Zeke said. "I quite like you." He rose to his feet. "Nation. Go tell Obadiah we're ready to go back to the ship. We will question her further there."

Nation complied and as soon as he was out of earshot, Zeke leaned in to whisper to me. "He is entirely on the side of Colonel Church. I am not. I will protect you as best I can, but we must continue to question you. I will pretend to be on his side, but please know that I am not. Abraham—I believe you know him? Your friend calls him Hammy?"

Again, I hoped my face gave no indications of yes or no.

"Abraham and I are... How shall I phrase this? Abraham and I are good friends of your friend, Edward."

An idea came into my mind right then. "So you will know something about Edward's mother."

Just then, I smelled smoke. Not the smoke of burning trees or houses or chickens or cows, the smell of tobacco. Not our tobacco smoke. The smoke of a Newcomer's pipe. A New England Newcomer. I did not let on that I had smelled it.

"Do you know something of Edward's mother?"

"I might."

"The last I heard, Edward was trying to convince his mother to travel from London to Boston. Either to live or to visit. Do you know if he has succeeded? And if so, which did he succeed in getting her to do? Move permanently? Or visit?"

"He has done neither. And I—"

"All right, then," came Obadiah's voice from the trees. "Let's get this boat in the water and get back to the ship. I'm starving."

"I am looking forward to a pint of cider myself," added Nation.

"I'm assuming tea for you, Miss?" Obadiah asked.

"That depends."

"On what?" asked Nation.

"On what you have that I can put into it to kill the taste."

Nation gasped, Obadiah smiled and Zeke laughed out loud.

Twenty-eight

Zeke was claiming that he knew my friend Edward well. My friend Edward used to be the surgeon at the fort in Port Royal. He was French. Not English. Not New Englander like he was pretending to be in Boston. Not only did he help Captain KrommeZee get freed slaves secretly—and safely—from Boston to our land, but he helped get information about the plans of Colonel Benjamin Church to our land, as well. Much of this information through me.

Could it be that Zeke was telling the truth? That he was also a spy? Like Edward? Could I trust him? Did I have a choice? Could Zeke be merely *acting* like he knew Edward personally? Was his friend? If they wanted information from me, this would be a good way to fool me into trusting at least one of them.

Nation and Obadiah stood by the boulders again but they did not sit. I rose to my feet.

Zeke went to the boat to remove the chopped-off branch. As he tossed it toward the trees, he asked, "Who did this?"

"I did," said Obadiah. "To hide the boat. That's what you told me to do."

"I told you to actually hide— Oh, never mind." Then Zeke turned to me. "We want information on Edward and on Captain KrommeZee. We know they are running slaves up here."

I tried to make myself look both angry and serious as I stared into the eyes of Zeke, then Obadiah, then Nation. I hoped this would keep my face from showing anything to them.

"You must know about this," said Zeke.

"I am certain she knows everything," said Obadiah.

"Are they that intelligent though?" asked Nation.

I pretended something had landed on the back of my hand so I could turn my face away from him because that hand was wanting to reach out and squeeze his throat.

"Do you know?" Zeke insisted.

"She has to know, Zeke. That nigger she's been with all the time lately would have told her. Would he not?" Nation took a step closer to me. "They seem to be close chums. That's not a wise thing for a female to do. Even your kind. Those black Devils are dangerous. Especially the males. Ask anyone. Befriending negroes, even in your own land—which won't be yours much longer, will it?—is not wise at all. No. Not wise at all."

"I'm not worried." I said this while leaning toward him, staring right down into his face.

Nation stepped back.

"We've successfully repulsed your English invasions for many winters. Even before my parents were born."

"Ah. But now we have Queen Anne on our side."

When Obadiah spoke to me, he spoke kindly. "We recommend you don't resist the English. We know what they are capable of."

What did Obadiah mean by that, I wondered. He had referred to the English as "they."

"Come along," said Zeke. "Let's get her into the boat and off we go toward some serious questioning."

"And she'll not be the only one questioned," came a voice from the trees.

Three men stood there. Two had muskets that were pointed at Zeke. The third was sucking smoke out of a curved pipe. That's what I had smelled.

"We've been watching you, my boy," said Pipe Man. "You think you could get away with this forever?"

The two men waved their muskets from Zeke to the boat, back and forth.

Zeke made a move for my munti which was still beside my leg, but instead of putting it into the boat, he swung it at the two men holding the muskets. He hit one of them on the head and the other ducked down.

"Here," he said, handing the munti to me. "Run."

I ran.

Twenty-nine

But I didn't run far. Where would I go? Would I lead these men back to Mak's village? Or to Flower Stalk's village? I could do neither. Of course I couldn't. I could not even play the role of the snipe as there was nowhere else to lead my pursuers away to. I knew they were close behind me, that I was visible to them. I knew that even if I leaped away to hide behind a tree or a boulder, they would see me do it.

There was no point in running.

I turned to face them.

***

We were all soon in the boat to be taken to the ship. Obadiah and Nation rowed. The men with the muskets kept them pointed at Zeke. Pipe Man sat there sucking on his pipe and staring at me.

On board, Pipe Man mumbled something and everyone scattered but Zeke and me, even the men with the muskets.

"Get below," he told Zeke. "You'll both be questioned."

***

Where Zeke had led me, I assumed were the captain's quarters. Why did I assume that? The cabin was spacious, there were shelves with many books, some of which I recognized the titles of—and this surprised me because Marguerite's books, and I read them all, were usually books written for women. But I suppose Marguerite's books were also for heroes. Was that why this captain had so many? Was he a romantic at heart? Would this mean, when he questioned us, he would be kind? Not threaten to throw us to the sharks and follow through with his threat? But I also saw a cabinet for alcohol sitting in one corner. Zeke went toward that one right away.

He poured something from one of the bottles into a small glass then waggled the glass in the air. "Yes?"

"No."

He added more to the glass then poured most of it down his throat. He made a face and coughed, but filled the glass again to the top. "There's nothing like Jamaican rum."

"Your captain doesn't mind people stealing his whiskey?"

"My captain doesn't *mind* anything these days. He's *out* of his mind."

"Is that a joke? If it is, I don't understand it."

"It's not a joke. He is out of his mind. He's delirious. That's why we brought you on board."

"App?"

"You haven't wondered why your medicine bag is still intact? Why we haven't searched you?"

Did I dare answer that question?

A rap at the door saved me from making a decision.

"Enter."

A man with a strange, puffy white hat and carrying a cloth-covered tray stepped inside. He placed the tray on the captain's bureau and removed the cloth. "It's the best we could do, Sir." The man left, closing the door quietly behind him.

"You're a sir," I said.

"More of a sir to some and less of a sir to others, I guess." Zeke removed a cup and a plate from the tray and set them on the bureau. "Grab that chair and pull it over."

I did.

Zeke went behind the bureau but didn't sit in the big chair there. Instead, he opened one of the drawers and removed two knives, two forks and two spoons. He divided these and with great care, placed them on each side of the plate on my side of the bureau. "Sit. Sit. I'll serve."

I sat.

"Are you hungry?"

"I'm not sure."

This made Zeke laugh. "She isn't sure if she's hungry or not. This woman is definitely amusing."

"I haven't been eating because I haven't had the desire to do so. I think that's called not having an appetite. But since I haven't been eating, then my body must be missing food, so would that be called hungry? Even if I don't feel it?"

"Either way, eat something. Give me your plate."

I did.

Zeke lifted one of the upside-down silver bowls off a plate on the tray. "Aha. Beans and fish. Yesterday we had fish and beans."

I couldn't help myself. I had to say something. "Variety in the diet is very important." But when I leaned in and the smell of it drifted up into my nose, I knew I would be going yet another day without eating. "Do you have tea?"

"Oh, tea. Yes. Of course, we have tea." He turned to remove two large mugs from a shelf in the wall behind him. With a napkin from the tray, he wiped both of them out then placed one on the bureau on the right side of the plate there, in front of me.

I looked up at him. He was smiling down at me.

He lifted a large pot with a spout from the tray and poured a good amount of what was in it in the mug. "Milk? Cream? Oh. Wait." He looked all over the tray, lifting napkins and plates here and there then said, "Looks like we are out. Sorry."

"I can do without it in my tea. I'm fine. But..."

"Yes? What else would you like?"

"Do you have sugar?"

Again, Zeke looked all over the tray. I knew that the cup he'd placed on the bureau had sugar cubes in it but I said nothing. Perhaps he wanted them for himself.

"Plain water would be fine," I said.

"Ah. Wait." He pulled out another of the drawers and came out with a tiny package of something wrapped in what looked like birch bark. "Here's some." With a grand sweep of his arm and hand, he placed this package beside my mug. "Open it."

I did.

"I prefer cane sugar," he said. "Others have less-sophisticated tastes, it seems."

I brought a small piece of the crumbly brown substance to my nose. It was maple sugar.

"Oh, thank you. Thank you." I dumped most of the maple sugar into my mug and took a grateful sip. The sugar had been successful. It had taken away the taste of their dreadful tea. "Thank you."

Zeke lifted the other upside-down silver bowl off its plate to reveal potatoes and some kind of meat. Using one of the forks and a knife from his belt, Zeke adjusted the meat on the tray and began to slice it.

"I don't mean to be impolite, but what is that?" I asked.

"I don't mind being impolite when Chef is not around to hear me. Do you want the truth?"

I nodded.

"I have no idea. It's probably some kind of fowl by the texture of it. A foul fowl perhaps? At least this one hasn't gone off. Thank God for that."

"You're not making my appetite improve any."

"I'm teasing you. We knew you were coming so we prepared something special for you."

This made thoughts race around in my head about stories that my friend Claude used to tell me about the Kings in his land, France. About people who wanted to be King poisoning people who were already King.

"Uh."

"Don't worry. It hasn't been poisoned." At this, he placed some of the meat onto his own plate. "I'll divide it evenly between us and I'll even take the first bite. How's that?"

"Have they…? What do they call it? Ah. Have they arrested us? And is this our last meal or something? We get to choose between suicide by food or by firing squad?"

"Edward is right about you. You are extremely and deliciously amusing."

"Everybody seems to be 'right' about me these days. Everybody else but myself." I couldn't help it, I began to cry.

"What's wrong. They aren't going to hurt you, believe it or not. They need you."

"They?"

"We. Do you want some of the fish?"

"No."

***

The meat was grouse and tasted good, but I have to tell you I didn't put any of it into my mouth until I saw Zeke do that, chew and swallow. He seemed to think that was funny. I didn't. We had only just finished the meal and were dabbing our lips with napkins when a rap sounded at the door.

Zeke leaned toward me over the bureau and spoke quietly to me. "To answer your question: She died years ago. In France. She was never in England." Then he said, "Enter."

At the door was Pipe Man and with him, was Hammy. Or perhaps it was the other way around because Hammy seemed to be in charge.

"Any luck getting information from her?" Hammy asked.

"Did you expect me to?"

Hammy smiled at me. "Let's get her settled in for the night." He turned to Zeke. "You realize we are going to be arresting you. Right?"

At this, Pipe Man stepped forward with a set of shackles. "Turn around."

"I should really be going," I said. "They'll be waiting for me. I have a husband to bury."

"I'm well aware of that," said Hammy. "My condolences. But I won't allow you to travel in the dark. Besides, they've gone on ahead."

The shackles clicked on Zeke's wrists.

"They said they'd wait for me." I wasn't certain if I was feeling anger, rejection or just the continuing sadness on missing Falcon.

"And they did. The one called Singing Bear was strongly torn between waiting for you and respecting the remains of your husband, but the final decision was made. They had no choice. They had to start back to Port Royal. And they did."

"Sorry for your loss, Missy," said Pipe Man as he led Zeke out the door, leaving me alone with the only person on this ship that I trusted.

"Can't you take me to shore? I need to be with Falcon."

"Falcon is gone. Deceased. He deserted you… What? … Six months ago?"

"Seven moons. And he and Solange didn't do anything with each other so he was still my husband."

"He deserted you."

"For a good cause."

"You have suitors. Two of them. And you have spent a night alone with at least one of them. Perhaps your heart has deserted him now too?"

"Nothing happened between me and Mak," I shot back at him.

Hammy smiled with one side of his mouth. "So I've heard."

"Stop that. It's not true."

"Which is not true? That you did? Or didn't?"

"I didn't. Stop thinking that I did. People are so… Oh."

"Let's go. You'll be staying in a different cabin for the night."

I rose from my chair.

"You'll have company."

I stepped away from him.

"Don't worry. They're female. And you won't be locked in. But I wouldn't try to leave, if I were you."

I heard a noise down the passageway and knew that Pipe Man was locking Zeke into another cabin.

"Will he be facing a firing squad?"

Hammy laughed. "No. He'll just be there for the night. To make it look good, you know?"

I didn't know.

As Hammy led me along the passageway, I asked him, "I thought, perhaps, you might have taken me to the one in charge. I was almost hoping it would be Benny."

"Benny? Oh, you mean Colonel Church."

"I guess that's what you people call him now. I was hoping he might have returned."

"He's been gone for months."

I actually wasn't hoping he had returned. I was wanting to imagine what his face would look like seeing me again ten years after he and I had had our differences. I liked to remember times like that. Times when someone who was doing a bad thing had that very same bad thing bounce back and do it to them.

"Here we are." Hammy tapped lightly on a door then opened it.

Inside the cabin were a woman of perhaps forty winters and a young girl, I would say, of twelve winters. They looked alike so I knew they were from the same family; and they were dressed like the Puritan women I had seen when I was in Boston Harbor. Boston Harbor, the last place I had seen Benny and the last place he had seen me. I thought it strange that these warring men would bring their wives and daughters with them.

In English I said to the woman, "Your husband has brought you and, I am assuming your daughter, along to war with him?"

The door clicked closed behind me.

"Je m'excuse. Je ne comprends pas l'angais."

In French, I replied. "I don't understand the English, either." I laughed but neither of them did. "Then why are you here?"

In a shaky voice, the young girl replied. "Maman and I are being kept prisoner."

"And we don't know why."

"Like I said. The English are difficult to understand. I don't even try anymore."

Not even a smile from either of them, but the woman spoke. "I am Rachelle. This is Yvonne."

"I am called Keskoua." I turned to reach for the cabin door's latch but the young girl was instantly at my side to put her hand over mine.

"No. Don't." This she said in a whisper. "There's a guard. See?" She pointed to the keyhole in the door then put her finger over her lips before she bent down to peer through the keyhole to show me how.

I did the same and with the sides of our heads touching, we looked through and there he was, on the other side of the passageway. He was young. Perhaps seventeen winters. He was standing, leaning against the far bulkhead with his eyes closed. I could only see him from the waist up, but I could tell by the way one arm slanted out that it was probably holding a musket.

The girl and I exchanged glances and I made the motion of a key turning in the lock as I put a question on my face. "I didn't hear him lock it."

The girl made the Sign of the Cross as she shook her head then looked up in the air with her hands pressed together. I was as thankful as she appeared to be that we hadn't been locked in. That Hammy had told the truth about that. I couldn't think of anything worse right then than being locked in a room in the hold of a ship that might at any moment be sunk by cannon shot.

I rose from my crouched position and began to look around the cabin. There were two sets of bunk beds, two portholes, a cabinet I knew would contain clothing, and other cabinets that would contain other objects. Combs and mirrors lay on a beautiful bureau with a mirror against the bulkhead.

I was about to look out the porthole when Rachelle asked.

"What's in your bag?"

"Why do you ask?"

"I had one very much like it, but when they took me, I didn't have it with me. Is it what I think it is?"

"What do you think it is?"

"She probably thinks it's a medicine munti," said Yvonne. "She is too afraid to ask in case you are one of their spies."

I laughed. "That makes us even, then."

"Have you eaten?" asked Rachelle. "We have. They usually feed us around this time. And leave us with tea." She motioned toward a large teapot with mugs beside it. "Would you like some tea?"

"Their tea tastes worse than moose brains."

Finally, laughter from both the woman and her daughter.

"This is usually the time they expect us to go to sleep. But first, I have a question."

"Ask."

"You wouldn't happen to be that famous healer from Port Royal, would you?"

"Famous? Really?"

"Yes. You're quite well-known. We heard all about your trip to Boston and how you saved Afia and Mak and Little Gracie. Are they still calling her Little Gracie? Or have they given her a name yet?"

"You know them?"

"Of course. Our villages are close and we would often trade among each other."

"Do you have a husband?"

"I did. His name was Lazare and he was killed by the Maudits anglaises."

"No, he wasn't. He was wounded, yes. But he is not dead."

A cry of joy came from the woman and she and her daughter embraced in tears.

"How do you know this?"

"They asked me to come help at your village and the village of Mak."

"Mak? Mak's village? What do you mean? Does this mean Chief Apistanewj…?"

"Mesgei´. Yes. He was killed. They asked Mak to take over as Chief."

"He's a good man."

"Yes. But now things have changed again and someone else has taken over."

Their faces asked the question.

"Matuwes is now Chief."

"Maman. That's that really strange one that was away, isn't it?"

"Yes," I said. "Let's speak no further of this. Let's get some sleep. I haven't slept for days but now I know I can."

***

The next morning, Yvonne and I looked through the keyhole to see the same young man in the same stance. Just before I turned away, I saw Zeke pass by. He and the young man greeted each other. Pipe Man was following Zeke.

"Is Zeke a good man or a bad man?"

"Depends on which side you're on," answered Rachelle. "Is he the one insisted you could keep your munti?"

"I don't know who made that decision. Or why. Everything seems strange to me. They said they were going to question me. They asked me about someone I know in Boston. They accused him…" and here, I smiled at Rachelle, "… of being a spy."

Rachelle leaned in close to me. "I think Zeke is a spy."

"I get the feeling none of them wants to be here. Zeke said something about needing me to help cure the captain of something."

"Oh, yes. Did he not tell you? That's why they took me and Yvonne. I'm a healer, too."

"Yes. Lazare said you were. He will be so relieved to know you both are unharmed."

"The captain was injured in one of the raids. His hand became infected and the poison is traveling up his arm. If it's not stopped, he will die."

"You couldn't help him?" I asked.

"I didn't have my munti. And they didn't trust me anyway. Especially the captain. He was calling me all manner of things. Witch. Devil. All the while, the poison was crawling from his finger to his hand then to his wrist. From what I hear, it's now creeping up his arm. And I hear, too, that his mind has become so confused, they think he will allow someone to help him. At least try to help him."

"Zeke said the same thing."

Just then, Yvonne slapped her hand over her mouth to stifle a squeal. There, behind her mother, at the porthole was a human face.

Rachelle spun.

I gasped then smiled. It was J-B. His smiling face was pushed aside and the face of Bear appeared with an even wider smile. Bear made a sign that we be quiet. All three of our heads bobbed up and down.

I pointed at the door behind me and made my mouth say, "There is a guard."

Bear made his mouth say, "We know."

His face disappeared.

Rachelle asked, "Do you know these men?"

"I most certainly do. They have come to get us out of here."

All the air seemed to go out of Yvonne as she collapsed onto the edge of the bed behind her.

"You will need to tell me what to expect. By that, I mean, explain your routine so we don't do anything to give my friends away. We must not vary from it."

"It's break-fast time. They will soon be bringing food."

"At least that's what they call it," said Yvonne, laughing. "Right?"

"How do they do that? I mean, who brings it in? And how? Is the food on a tray? Does one person bring it in while that guard stands at the door? Do they close the door behind them until they place the food…" I pointed to the small table in the corner of the room closest to the porthole. "There? Is that where they put it? Or do they hand it to one of you?"

"Someone brings it in, yes," said Rachelle. "It's on a tray. They do not close the door. The guard stands there."

"Where you saw him," Yvonne added. "Leaning against the wall like he is now. He doesn't seem to pay much attention to anything."

"And the one who brings it in says nothing, just places the tray on the table and leaves. He doesn't even speak to the guard."

A slight smile appeared on Yvonne's face. "Maman and I have made a joke about him. We have heard stories from some of the dark-skinned people that Captain KrommeZee brings to our land. They have told us of voodoo masters who use something from a special fish to kill a person, but he isn't really killed, he just seems that way. Then they wake him up again and he acts just like the man who brings our food in." She giggled. "I can't remember what they call them, but it doesn't matter. It helps Maman and me to not be so afraid."

From somewhere on the other side of the door, I heard a commotion. I heard English words that I knew had to be coming from the young guard. "I say, you can't come down here."

Then I heard Bear's voice and along with it—and this I could not believe—Second Son's voice, too. They sounded drunk.

From Second Son, in English, "We were informed by Benny—"

From Bear, in English, "Your illustrious leader."

"That since we have been of such benefit to your cause—"

"That we have helped tremendously, and that's exactly what he said. That's the word he used. 'Tremendously.' That we have helped tremendously toward the cause—"

"So we can have as many bottles of whiskey as we can carry."

I was immediately on my knees at the keyhole.

I saw Bear put his arm across Second Son's shoulders. "Well actually he said we could have three bottles each."

"That's what I said. As many as we can carry."

I rose to my feet so we were all facing the door when the latch clicked and moved and the door started to open, I think we all held our breath.

From the side of my mouth, I whispered to Rachelle and Yvonne. "Those are my friends. Don't be afraid. But be ready to act."

Yvonne shuffled close to me and slipped her arm through mine and her mother, on the other side of her, shuffled close, too.

I heard the guard's voice. "What are you doing? No, no. Don't do that. You can't go in there."

"Too late," said Bear, just as the door swung open. This allowed us to see Bear leap toward the guard's musket and remove it from his hand. "Stay quiet. I don't want to hurt you."

I was surprised to see that Second Son was not nearly as drunk as he had sounded. Lithe as a tqoqwej, a wild cat, he leapt into our room. To Rachelle and Yvonne he said, "Get those dresses off." To me he said, "Help them. And be quick about it."

I could hear Bear giving instructions to the guard in the hall. "The native woman is my wife. I will kill you if you do anything that will cause her harm."

Rachelle and Yvonne were soon freed from their bulky dresses and were standing there, still fully covered, but in only two layers.

"And while we're at it," Bear continued, "we will take these two ladies as well. And you're going to help us."

The guard cleared his throat and tried to look stern when he spoke. "I'll have you know—"

"No. We'll have *you* know that you are going to do exactly as we tell you. We have sent a pigeon message to our *compadres* in your village—yes, in your home village in New England—and unless they receive another one, and soon, your mother and your sisters will be tortured and killed." I knew Bear well enough to catch the slight change in his voice that told me this was as far from the truth as it could be.

Behind me, I heard the sound of cloth being ripped. I turned to see that Second Son was using his knife and his hands to tear the Puritan dresses into strips.

The guard's face suddenly went pale and he stammered, "Whatever you wish. Please. Please don't harm my family. What do you want me to do?"

Second Son reached for my arms and pulled them behind my back. With one of the strips from the dresses, he loosely tied my wrists together. He leaned forward between me and Yvonne to whisper, "Don't be afraid. This is part of the plan."

Second Son then tied Yvonne's wrists, then Rachelle's.

"Ready here, sir," he said in a loud voice.

Bear poked the guard's musket into his side and said, "You will lead us up onto the deck where you will approach your captain and tell him that you have just received secret instructions from…" He turned to me. "He's not called 'Benny.' What's his real name?"

"Church. Colonel Benjamin Church."

"… from Colonel Church himself that he wishes to question these women as he has learned they have information he requires."

Our guard did as he was told.

***

Once on deck, I learned that Zeke had not lied about this ship's captain. Captain was in no condition to agree or disagree with anything. The tide was coming in, and fast, making the ship sway, and every time it swayed, a cry of pain came from the bundle of blankets on the deck up by the ship's wheel.

The guard said, "Captain was injured in our last foray. He is suffering the effects."

Without thinking, I said, "I have my munti. I'll see if I can help him."

From the bundle of blankets on the deck up by the ship's wheel came a weak voice. "Over my dead body will I ever have a heathen ministering to me."

Zeke appeared beside me. "Looks like he may get his wish if he doesn't change his attitude about you people. Are you willing to help him anyway?"

"They set you free?"

"Without Captain in control, anything can happen. Are you going to answer me? Are you willing to help him?"

Before I could answer, the guard replied, "These fellows are saying that the Colonel wants to see these women. Apparently, they have information." He glanced at Bear. "Valuable information."

The bundle of blankets on the deck beside the ship's wheel muttered, "He's back? Very well, then. Release them."

One of the soldiers near the ship's rail looked over the side. "There's a Frenchman in a boat down here. Halt!"

I recognized J-B's voice. "Je suis ici pour rassembler les femmes. J'ai été envoyé par Monsieur le Colonel."

"What's that devil saying?"

J-B said more but I didn't hear it all.

The man hanging over the rail said, "Something about… He's here to collect the women… He… He was sent by the Colonel. He's to take them to Port Royal. To a ship that waits there. One of ours, he says. So I don't recommend you shoot him."

The bundle of blankets on the deck beside the ship's wheel moaned. Zeke went quickly up to the bundle and knelt there.

I glanced over to the ship's upper rail to see both Nation and Obadiah standing there. Obadiah leaned toward Nation to whisper something to him. Something Nation didn't like, by the way he reacted.

Zeke leaned in speak to the captain. "I would not be too quick to refuse the services of this healer. Something tells me she is good at what she does. We can let the other women go. We'll have this one remain to tend to your wound. I'll take her ashore later. We know nothing about treating wounds such as yours, Sir. As you are no doubt aware. Sir. You know yourself it has festered and needs attention."

I still had not seen Captain's face, but I knew by a slight movement at one end of the bundle of blankets that he had nodded consent.

Zeke motioned me up near the ship's wheel.

"We are not leaving without my wife being with us," said Bear as he climbed over the rail. "Forget him."

"No. I will not do that," I said, kneeling beside the bundle of blankets. "Let me look at him. Perhaps I can deal with this quickly."

Zeke called out, "She'll be safe with me. Go. Go now before Captain changes his mind."

Bear said something to the others who were already in the boat. He raised his hand to me and disappeared over the rail.

As soon as I saw the captain's hand, I knew why he was so ill. Part of one finger was missing, no doubt from a musket ball. The flesh around the wound was red and black and smelled like death. Yellow slime oozed from its edges. As gently as possible, I pulled away the lacy frills at the end of his jacket sleeve.

"Please cut open his sleeve."

Zeke pulled out a knife and did as I requested.

I was expecting what I saw, so I was able to keep my face the same. I was happy to see that the red streaks there were only up to the elbow.

"When was Captain injured?"

Nation was the one to answer. "I think it was a few days ago? It was early in the morning, I know that much."

"Do you have garlic on board?"

"I'll ask Chef," said Zeke, who clambered down the ladder then into the hold.

I called out after him. "And honey. Ask if he has honey."

Zeke's head poked out from the hold. "And?"

"Any kind of fruit, especially the juice. And clean cloths. Tell him to boil the cloths."

Nation knelt down beside me which made me lean away from him.

"Or maybe it was two mornings ago," he said. "Five? Ten? I get confused sometimes." I noticed that he glanced over at Obadiah who shot his chin out at him, telling him to keep talking.

I could smell Nation's breath. "I know rum can make a person feel better about things. But after a while, it does the opposite. If you don't mind my saying so. If you don't mind me giving you advice—and believe me, I know what I'm talking about—I would recommend you consume less of it."

Nation nodded. "It's not easy, you know, when everybody else is doing it."

"You strike me as a person who does not like to go along with everybody else. Am I right?"

"You strike me as a person..." His eyes went to where Obadiah was standing. Somewhat loudly—loud enough for Obadiah to hear—he said, "I'm sorry. I'm sorry what I said to you. I'm sorry I called you a christly devil. But don't tell Zeke I said that. I don't want him thinking I'm... that

I'm weak."

I smiled at him, but I don't think that made him feel any better. "Your secret is safe with me."

Again, his eyes went to Obadiah and he spoke loudly enough for him to hear. "I have a reputation to maintain."

"As do I."

In no time, Zeke had returned with Cook at his side, both of them with their hands full of what I had requested.

Cook handed me a bundle of cloths. "I always keep a boiled supply on hand. We are at war, aren't we?"

"It seems we are."

On the skin my munti sat on, I placed the jar of honeycomb, several heads of garlic, a large mug of what smelled bitter and sweet at the same time. "What's this?"

"Juice from oranges," answered Cook. "They come from the West Indies. Are you not familiar with them?"

"I've heard of them but have not used their juices." I tipped the mug slightly to have some of the juice flow onto my hand. I tasted it. "It tastes like it has many valuable properties. Yes. Ensure that Captain drinks plenty of this. Now, each of you, please pay attention to what I am about to do."

Zeke, Nation and Cook leaned over me while I tended to the Captain's wound.

"This must be done four times every day until this red line…" I pointed to it. "… goes away. That will be your signal. And you must not only put crushed garlic and honey on his wound…" I showed them how. "But you must get him to eat foods with honey and garlic in them."

I dug into my munti and brought out a package of tea which I handed to Cook.

"Tea. It's tea. It will help." I turned toward Nation when I said this next part. "It is a good idea to keep him from drinking any spirits unless his pain becomes too unbearable."

"If that's all," said Cook. "I have a pot on the stove I must tend to."

I thanked him.

"They've lowered the boat," said Zeke, pointing at two men holding ropes at the rail.

Nation helped me to my feet. "Let me help you with that bag of yours."

I allowed Nation to carry my munti to the rail where a ladder led down to the boat that bobbed in the waves. I threw my leg over the rail.

Nation took my elbow and leaned close to me. "I meant it when I said I was sorry. Can you forgive me? I was wrong. I am ashamed."

"There is no need to be ashamed about doing something we didn't know was wrong. The shame should come from knowing but doing anyway."

He turned his face away from me then, but not soon enough because I saw water forming at the corner of the eye closest to me. I think he didn't want me to see that.

I patted his arm. "Maybe some day, when all this is over, you and I can have a cup of tea together and I'll tell you all the things I've been wrong about."

I crawled down the ladder to the boat below. Zeke was right behind me.

"Safe voyage," said Nation.

"And a safe voyage to you," I called up to him. "But make sure he drinks my tea, not yours. E´e?"

Nation turned to Obadiah who was now watching down from beside Nation. "She's really funny if you pay attention to her. Quite the delight, actually."

Thirty

The sea was steady while Zeke rowed me to shore where the others had waited for me.

"Are you certain they will not hang you or shoot you for being a spy?" I asked Zeke. "You can always come with us."

"Nobody cares anymore. I'll be fine," he said. "There are some who are eager to take over your land but there are just as many of us who aren't. It was an opportunity to earn some money. Good money. Most of the men on my ship have nothing against the French or the Indians."

"So I don't have to worry about you?"

"Not at all. Except, perhaps, one thing."

I waited.

"Now that I have money in my pockets, I will be asking a certain young woman to be my wife. I think I will need a lot of prayers to help me deal with that." He laughed.

"Not all marriages are prisons."

"She is the sister of Nation."

"Oh."

**

I knew from what Zeke had told me and from what I had heard and seen, that there would be no trouble this time from the Maudits anglaises as we traveled to Flower Stalk's village, but we separated into groups and took the long way around through the bush anyway, just in case.

Second Son and I traveled together. It was his idea. He said nothing, but I knew he wanted to talk to me. I could feel it. I had strong suspicions that Agada was behind this. I could almost hear her voice in my head: *If you are going to be helping Keskoua, try to be alone with her so you can talk.* But I said nothing to him and he said nothing to me. I would have to wait.

***

Second Son and I arrived at the village and I was happy to see a small fire boiling water for tea. I thought we were the first, but J-B was there, washing his hands at the edge of the bay.

I was both surprised and not surprised to see Pierre there, seated cross-legged beside Flower Stalk.

"I hope Gabbie set you free and you didn't desert your post," I said to him.

"I was reassigned. To this village."

"That's convenient. For how long?"

"Permanently."

I laughed. "What's the word for that? I should know but I can't remember."

"Népotisme," said Francine who was standing behind him.

Flower Stalk rose to come hug me. "Please, please. Join us. We have biscuits. Actual biscuits. Gisèlle got them. They're wonderful with tea."

Laughing, Gisèlle announced, "I stole them. That's why they taste so good."

"From where?" I asked.

"When they were watching us, I watched them."

Flower Stalk said. "That's the benefit of dealing with people who think they're superior. They assume certain things. Gisèlle watched and waited until the man on guard duty had too much tea so went into the trees to relieve himself. Then she sneaked in to steal the man's food. She made it look like it was an animal. She did this several times to several guards."

Flower Stalk sat down again, patting the ground beside her on the other side of Pierre. "Please be seated, Keskoua."

Dit Ça and Otter were already seated. Although there was plenty of room for me, Dit Ça moved over more, so Otter slid over, too. I knew this was out of respect.

"Welaliog."

They bowed their heads to me.

"Is this everyone? No. Where is Lazare?"

J-B said, "He's over here."

Lazare's voice came from somewhere near J-B. "Can a man not piss without having someone wonder where he is?"

Francine said, "I am sorry about your husband. I am especially sorry to hear you could not be there when they…"

"He's buried and with great respect, a Sacred Fire and a ceremony." said J-B. "Please do not increase Keskoua's grief by adding guilt to it."

"M'excuse. Sorry," said Francine, her face and body not showing it. "Why am I the one always having to say I'm sorry about something?"

Then Bear's voice reached my ears, too. "Yes. We held the ceremony. Everyone came. Even some of the soldiers from the fort came to pay their respects and to wish him well on his Journey."

I felt J-B's kind hand on my shoulder as he passed behind me to enter the circle. I couldn't help myself. Water came out of my eyes.

Bear was instantly pushing Dit Ça over to squeeze in beside me, crossing his legs and placing his arm over my shoulders. This made everyone else move over, too. "You couldn't do anything about it, oqoti."

"Oqoti?" muttered Francine as she adjusted her clothing and got her legs crossed again. She and Gisèlle were on the other side of the circle by now. "He's using special terms of endearment now. I wonder how that's going to work when Mak finds out."

"How do you know about that?" Gisèlle whispered to her.

"Same way you know, I guess."

Bear snapped at them. "Stop it, you two!"

Lazare pushed himself in between Dit Ça and Otter. This made everyone move again. J-B slid in between Otter and Gisèlle. This closed the circle.

"Before we get started, may I ask a question?"

"Certainly, Keskoua," said Flower Stalk. "Go ahead. What is it?"

"It took us several days to get here from Port Royal. How were you able to get back there, with a heavy travois, with Solange who is not able to walk well, hold a Sacred Fire and a ceremony for Falcon, and then get back here in… What? Less than two days? How did you get there and back so fast?"

"We ran into Klu," said J-B. "But he didn't eat us. Instead he flew us there and back."

Bear's eyes told him he wasn't pleased with J-B's response.

The others tried not to laugh.

J-B shrugged. "By boat."

"Klu doesn't use boats," said Otter. "You sure it wasn't the Sabawaelnu?"

And this made even Bear laugh.

"Who?" asked Dit-Ça.

"Water spirits," Otter told him.

"Ah. I missed so much learning being away learning things of no value. Didn't I?"

Otter caressed Dit Ça's back. "It's na to´q. Ça va bien, oui? Don't concern yourself. You just now learned something you didn't know. Didn't you?"

Bear said. "The Big Bay is within walking distance. Easy walking distance. There's a boat. With oars, sails and two Acadian boys hidden there. They've started their own business transporting people along the east shore of the Big Bay."

"That's right," J-B said. "And now, since all the Maudits anglaises' ships are gone—all but one, that is, and that one is disabled because its captain is disabled—it's much safer again to go on the Big Bay."

"To where we must be getting and soon. Yes?" Bear did not take his eyes from J-B's face.

"Yes. They rely on the tides."

Flower Stalk motioned to Gisèlle who reached into a bag hanging from her waist to take out a bundle of leaves wrapped around something. She spread the leaves to show several biscuits lying there. She was laughing as she put some of them back into her bag. "I have only eleven so we'll have to break them apart and share. But that's better than no biscuit at all, isn't it?"

"What do you mean *only* eleven?" asked Lazare, his eyes moving around the circle. "There are ten of us here. Second Son has disappeared. And you put some back."

"That's not true," said Flower Stalk.

Then everyone was looking at Lazare and laughing.

He leaned down to adjust the front of his trousers. "What? Is something hanging out? Why are you all laughing at me?" He rose to his feet. He was angry. "Stop staring at me. Right now. Stop it."

Then Second Son's voice came from near the guaq. "Turn around, Lazare. Look what we found."

Lazare's eyes moved before his head did and his head moved before his body did. But when he turned and saw Rachelle and Yvonne standing there, one on either side of Second Son, a gasp came from, I'm certain, his very heart.

"Yes, it's true," said Rachelle. "We're alive. And so are you."

Laughing, Gisèlle took the extra biscuits from her bag. "We had you going, didn't we?"

Thirty-one

As we walked along the trail toward the Big Bay, Second Son and I had stayed together and let Bear and J-B walk ahead. I was not surprised he opened up to me the way he did. I knew he had been wanting to. And he didn't once call me Oh Great Healer.

"Of course, I'm afraid to go through it again. I think that's part of why I have been avoiding it."

"It'll be easier this time, Second Son. You won't be going through this alone."

"I wish you wouldn't call me that."

"What? Second Son? Do you want to tell me why?"

"I don't like it. That's why. Could you perhaps call me Secky? Like Agada does?"

"It will take some practice but yes."

He kept his face turned away from mine so I couldn't read his reaction to anything.

"Why does the name Second Son bother you so much?" I could imagine being called "Second" anything would have made a child feel... Well. Second. A failure? But I wanted to hear it from him. I wanted *him* to hear it from him.

"My brother called me that all the time. Except he called me Second Best. My father would admonish him every time he heard him say it, but

209

that didn't stop him. He just called me that behind our father's back then. And more often."

I dug into my munti and handed him a sweet. I still had some left.

"He was not even my father's son but let me know every day that he was going to be Chief anyway. He was the first born. Wela´lin, Keskoua. These sweets are good. Maybe I will become attached to them instead of to whiskey, e´e?"

"I don't understand. What do you mean, he wasn't your father's son? Your mother was a loyal woman. Your father was the only man she was ever with."

"Do you not remember what happened to you? And how Claude claimed the baby as his own? To save your—"

"We're talking about you. Remember? Not me."

"Oh. Have I hit a soft spot in someone's memory?"

"Yes. Now please continue. Why do you hate the name Second Son?"

"Why wouldn't anyone hate that name. And the Grandfathers and Grandmothers would not give me another. No matter how much I begged them."

"I don't believe that. Why would they not give you a name? Never? They never even offered to give you one after your Spirit Quest?"

"I did not go on a Spirit Quest."

This took the breath out of me and I tripped over a tree root.

Second Son—Secky—had his hand out under my elbow quick as a sqolj's tongue, a frog's tongue.

"You didn't? Why not?"

"My brother again. He interfered with everything. Every time I mentioned it, he would cause some kind of chaos to draw attention away from me toward himself so people would forget. Even my parents forgot. When he went too far that time and got himself killed, even I forgot."

"I heard about that. Very sad. You say he brought it upon himself?"

"Not intentionally, Keskoua. He wasn't crazy. Just mean."

"How could he have had such power over you?"

"I allowed it, didn't I? Instead of standing up for myself, I decided to hide myself in a fog. He didn't have power over me, I did. Speaking of which…" At this, Second Son reached into the bag on his shoulder to bring out a small bottle, like the small bottles Pierre carried with him.

"Let me guess. Pierre?"

"Pierre. Sorry. I have to take some of this. I am starting to shake. I will be happy to get back home so I can start to stop." He laughed. "Start to stop. How silly."

"You need to be kinder to yourself, Second—uh, Secky. Look. We're here. Oh. What an unusual boat."

Bear and J-B were already aboard the craft. It was large and flat with square front and back ends and I could tell there were places to hide people—and objects? Objects like weapons and ammunition?

The two boys, perhaps nineteen winters old and looking as unlike each other as I have ever seen—even more different than Agada and Solange—were smiling and holding out their hands toward me and Second Son. One boy had similar features to Mak, but his skin was not nearly as dark. The other had eyes that were narrow slits and his skin was a pale golden shade. His hair was as black as black could be and straight. He wore it tied up on top of his head. Bear had said they were Acadian, and they spoke French the same way as Acadians did, so I knew they were from our land. But I'd never seen anyone like them before. They were quite handsome so I imagined there would be children like them everywhere in no time at all. Especially since they had their own business, too, and could afford to raise a family.

Second Son grasped my arm and pulled me away. He spoke quietly. "I have something to say."

"Yes?"

"About Bear."

"What about him?"

"Coming from me, you may not believe it but his intentions toward you are not entirely… What's the word? Honorable. That's it. His intentions are not entirely honorable."

"Come on, you two. Let's go." This was J-B. "Tide's starting to go out."

"He likes you, yes. He respects you. Who doesn't?"

"You?"

"That's not funny and I'm sorry, na to´q? I'm serious here. Listen to me. He wants you as his woman."

"He's made that obvious but—"

"Come on!" This time it was Bear calling out.

"*Jésus Christ*, Second Son! Are you trying to get us killed?" This from J-B.

"Il a raison. He's right. We devons aller now." This was one of the boys.

"He wants you by his side. Yes. Not so much for love, but for what you can offer as support to him. With him as Chief and his woman as the healer and storyteller, he will have complete power over everyone."

Second Son made sense, but I didn't trust him on this. "And you especially wouldn't like that. You still want to be Chief, don't you?"

"I won't be living in our village anymore. I will be living with Agada. She will be my woman. At least she said she would be. Or maybe that's just because she's afraid of me. Afraid to say no. Do you think so?"

"I think she likes you and respects you very much and would be happy having you as her man. Especially if you can give up the whiskey."

He held his hands up. They were shaking. "I have no ulterior motives regarding Bear. And it's not if I give up the whisky, it's when."

"You realize, of course that—"

"Yes, yes. I know. Matuwes is Chief there. I will not interfere. In fact, I will do my best to support her."

Several voices now: "Come on, you two. Venez! Maintenant!"

"But Mak is another story," whispered Second Son.

By this time, J-B had hold of my upper arm and was dragging me away with him.

"What about Mak? Is he the same way in your jealous mind?"

"Come on, Keskoua. You can talk on the boat."

Despite my protests, J-B had me on the boat. Second Son was right behind me.

We all settled ourselves into the strange craft, the boys let the sails go, then Golden Skin was at the oars and Light Dark-Skin was at the rudder. The tide was fast and the motion of the boat lulled me to sleep, so for me, we were on shore near Port Royal in what seemed to be no time at all. I was so exhausted, I didn't even care that Second Son had not had a chance to answer my question about Mak. Whether Mak's intentions were "honorable" or not. I was so exhausted, I didn't care about anything. I just wanted to be home.

"Right through here," said Bear, pointing to a path into the bush. "But I recommend, when we get close to the fort, you make all the noise you can, both talking and walking, in case they have a guard who startles easily."

"That's not funny," said J-B.

"Did he tell you he almost got his head shot off last time, oqoti?"

"Don't call me that. I am not your woman."

Thirty-two

Gabbie was one of the first to greet us and he pulled me aside to say that the pigeon messages from Edward had resumed and that he was "frantic" to hear from me.

Behind Gabbie, a soldier stood with a musket in one hand and a cage with two pigeons in the other. Behind him, two more soldiers held similar cages.

"Set that down beside Madame Keskoua," he told the first soldier, who did as he was told. Then to me, Gabbie said, "I recommend, before you are swamped with bienvenus, you send off a message to him."

"But I—"

Gabbie reached into one of his pockets and removed strips of birch bark. From another pocket, he took a small bottle of what I knew was ink, then from inside his jacket, appeared a quill. "No excuses, Keskoua. Write to him now. He's extremely worried about you." He removed the top from the ink bottle and held it out so I could dip the quill into it.

With my munti hanging off one shoulder and another bag hanging off each arm, I scribbled a quick message.

Home. Safe.

When I looked up, Gabbie was dangling thread and one of the other soldiers was pointing a pigeon's leg at me.

I wrapped the note around the pigeon's leg, wished it good speed and off it went.

Thirty-three

Over the next while, nothing much had changed at Port Royal or at my village except that Mak had arrived much earlier than expected and he and I had made something of a commitment to each other. I say something of a commitment because I had refused to sleep in his wikuom or allow him to sleep in mine. For one thing, I had to spend all my time at the special cabin in the bush with Second Son while he got free of the whiskey that was living inside him. And for another thing, I wasn't sure I could allow a man to touch me in that special way. Like I said before, it was different with Falcon. I don't know why, but it was. I hadn't had the same fear of him as I had of other men. Maybe it was because Falcon knew exactly what had happened between me and Father Soucy that time, when I was only fifteen winters old, knew what Father Soucy had done to me, putting a baby, my daughter Jeanne, inside me without my consent. Mak knew some had happened but until I could tell him everything, and I mean everything, I could not let him to be with me in that way. He had to be told. By me. First.

Within half a moon, Second Son had gotten through his withdrawal from whiskey without damage to either his body or his mind and was about to head off to live in Matuwes's village with Agada. She had been sending pigeon messages every day, but I hadn't told him about them until he was close to the end of his ordeal, around the time when he was about to give up because it was taking so long and was still so difficult to do. Agada's messages had given him strength to keep going. He was now certain he would be doing the right thing by moving to the village where Matuwes was Chief. He was not so certain anymore of his "power"—as he called it, but while laughing at himself when saying it—over Agada. "That will be up to her," he informed me.

During the times of his withdrawal, when his head was clear and we were filling in the time before his next bout of visions and seizures might start up again, I asked him if he would like to talk about Falcon. About why Falcon had gone back to the drink. Why Second Son had gone back to the drink as well. I also wanted to know how Second Son and Agada had made such a strong connection.

"It wasn't me and it wasn't him who got the other one going," Second Son told me. "It was the circumstances. It was from what happened. It was from how we met the girls. I mean Solange and Agada. And no. I am not blaming them for getting Falcon and me back drinking whiskey. Something happened."

"Do you want more tea?" I asked him.

"I'm fine. No. Yes. Give me more. Fill up my mug. Please."

I did.

"Falcon and I were in the bush. We were on the hunt for the places the Maudits anglaises were hiding their guards. We had already been on a successful food hunt for rabbits, so were also looking for a clearing to set a fire ablaze to cook them.

"We heard a sound up ahead. It was quite the commotion. Men crying out, women crying out. And you know Falcon, any time a woman is in distress, he is there. Actually…" And here, Second Son wiped wetness from one of his eyes. "… any time a man, woman or child is in distress, Falcon is… was… there. As you know."

I nodded.

"We approached quietly to see three coureurs du bois beating on a gentleman—we could see he was a gentleman by his clothing, his boots, his hat, his trimmed facial hair. He was French. Probably from Île-Royale by his accent and demeanor. We knew instantly that this man was being robbed for his purse. One of the coureurs took out his knife and pierced the man's chest with it. The man was down instantly.

"That's when we heard a woman's scream. That's when we saw Solange and Agada cowering in the trees. Their legs were tied by ropes to each other and to the tree.

"'Shut your whoring mouths,' the man with the knife told them. 'Or you are next.'

"His companions laughed. 'I'm quite done with both of them,' said one of the others. 'Now that we have gold, we can purchase the services of better than these. Some with hair.' The others laughed at this. Solange had already tried to hide her flaming hair by cutting it off at the roots, hoping to be less noticeable.

"The gentleman was obviously dead because he made no sound or movement when they cut off two of his fingers to remove his rings. Another of the men, the one who had said he was done with them, withdrew his knife, too, and approached Solange.

"At this, Falcon leaped toward him, with his own knife drawn, and slit the man's throat. I was right behind him and we had soon killed all three of these men and set the girls free of their bonds.

"The girls were grateful of course and I did not say no to Agada when she thanked me in her special way. Solange neither offered nor did Falcon ask for a similar favor. You have to know he and Solange did not ever…"

"I know."

"But soon, Falcon began to have regrets."

"Regrets?"

"Regrets for having taken the lives of those men. It didn't bother me in the slightest. They deserved it. But you know Falcon. A kinder man never existed. He never judged anyone. Good or bad."

"That's what drove him back to the whiskey?"

"That's what drove both of us back to the whiskey. Seeing him turn off the whole world like that, the way I used to do, the way he and I both used to do…"

"I understand," I said. "More tea?"

"Please."

"You did the right thing, you know. Saving those women."

"Thank you, Keskoua. Thank you for being who you are."

Thirty-four

Second Son and I were waiting near the fort for one of Captain KrommeZee's ships to dock. Second Son would be taking it to the next port where Agada would be waiting for him. I could already see several dark-skinned passengers leaning against the rail, their smiles wide and relaxed. It was good that Captain KrommeZee was able to travel back and forth to Boston again, even though I knew in my heart that it wouldn't last for long. I'd had a dream. A melgwisgat, un cauchemar, a nightmare. I had dreamed there would be no more French spoken in our land. And no more dark-skinned freed slaves.

Behind us I heard a cry, "Ow. Maudit tabernac." It was Mak. I think he would be using French at certain, special times for the rest of his life no matter what happened.

I heard J-B laugh. "You have to keep your eye on the nail you are hammering, Mak. Not on Keskoua."

"It's not easy," he said, waving his hammer and his hand in the air and calling out to me, "I'm fine. No damage done."

I waved back.

Mak was building his inn and J-B was helping him, along with my brother, Gig, and others from our village. Even some of the soldiers from the fort were helping out. Were they hoping Mak's whiskey, wine and beer would be superior to what their own tavern offered?

220

I know the *food* at Mak's inn would be better. Solange would be the chef and was already taking lessons from Marguerite, Claude's wife. Yes. Marguerite's romance books were once again arriving from Boston. But she was also receiving books about cooking from France, too.

At first, there had been great concern about Solange's disease, sa grande vérole. But the surgeon at the fort had provided some foreign cure for it—one that had almost killed her but appeared to have worked. She told me she would continue to act as though infected even though she was having no more discomfort or signs, so I was comfortable with that. Some weren't, of course, but in every community, every society, there are always those who like an excuse to hate another. I'll never understand why.

"You never did answer my question about Mak. Did you?" I asked Second Son.

"I didn't need to, did I?"

That was true. There had been no need to answer my question about Mak. I knew the answer. Mak was a good man. His intentions toward me were honorable. He had been patient with me, taking great care not to in the slightest way force himself on me. We still had not consummated—as the Fathers called it—our relationship, but that would happen soon enough. He had told me that once his inn was built, that when our special "appartemente des aubergistes" the owners' apartment, was completed, we would move in there and begin our lives together officially. I think that's why he kept hammering his thumb and fingers, he was rushing too much.

And Bear was…

What was Bear? Poor Bear. Bear was furious that Mak had moved to Port Royal, that was no surprise. But now that my intentions had been made clear that I had no interest in being Bear's woman, there was no shortage of… I had even asked Marguerite what the word would be for women wanting a specific suitor to approach them, would it be a suitoree?

but she just laughed and said, "They will fight among themselves and he will no doubt choose the victrix."

"The what?"

"The victrix. That's feminine for victor."

"I'm surprised your head isn't the size of a whale's, Marguerite. It holds so much information."

"I love you, too, Keskoua." And she hugged me. "You've made the right choice."

Acknowledgments

Special thanks go to Phyllis Bohonis, Evelyn Crete, Catina Noble, Sue Pictou and the Online Talking Dictionary: www.mikmaqonline.org/.

About the Author

Sherrill Wark is a former editor who designs print/digital books for indie authors. She's the author of: *How to Write a Book: Park It, Get to Work*, *Transplanted Heads: Your Muse Can't Write Worth Sh*t*, and *90 Steps to the Base Camp of Conscious Awareness* (non-fiction); *Death in l'Acadie: a Kesk8a story* and *Refuge in l'Acadie: a Kesk8a story* (the first two of a planned 6-book historical fiction series) *Graven Images* (fiction); *Vivie Goes to Hell in a Hatchback* (YA); *Mostly of Love & the Perils Thereof: The Sequel* and *The Closet Hides a Set of Stairs* (poetry). Under her pseudonym Christina Crowe, she has published *A Girl Dog's Breakfast*, scary stories and rude poems and *The Unkindest Cut: Short Creepy Movie Scripts*. Sherrill is also a screenwriter and has finished three screenplays: *The Soul Eaters* (Sci-Fi), *Skin Eater* (serial killer stuff), and *The Bus to Lo Siento* (drama) which landed in the top 10% (out of 600) in the 2013 Oaxaca Film Fest.

On her paternal grandmother's side, she is an Acadian descendant of Claude Guidry and Marguerite Petitpas.

Characters

Afia—escaped "slave", sister of Mak, mother of Little Gracie

Agada—Second Son's young girlfriend, short pale-yellow hair, palest blue eyes

Apistanewj—Chief Apistanewj, former (killed) chief of Mak's village

Benny—slave hunter from New England, Colonel Benjamin Church (real-life character, leader of the New England Rangers)

Big Bay—Bay of Fundy

Big Meadow—Grand Pré

Captain KrommeZee—captain of the *Rita Petronella*, "underground railroad" ship

Caetano—Matuwes's drug deal/boyfriend

Celeste—a resident of Mak's village

Claude Guidry—friend of Keskoua; husband of Marguerite Petitpas (the author's 7th great-grandfather)

Damnation—Nation, man who captures Keskoua

Dit Ça—Acadian man in Flower Stalk's village

Dit Ceci—Acadian woman in Flower Stalk's village, a.k.a. Matuwes

Edward Gooden—formerly known as Monsieur Hermel St-Amand, previous surgeon at the fort, now living in Boston as Edward Gooden

Falcon—Keskoua's husband

Flower Stalk—the new Chief of Mtaban

Gabbie Grenier – soldier at Port Royal in *Refuge in l'Acadie*, now in a
high position at the fort

Geneviève—friend and teacher of Keskoua

Gi´gwesu—a.k.a. Gig, Keskoua's brother

Gisèlle—survivor at Mak's village

Gracie Waite—owner of the Blind Pig Inn in Boston (*Refuge in l'Acadie*)

Hammy, Abraham—soldier/guard, friend of Agada

J-B—son of Claude and Marguerite (the author's 6th great-granduncle)

Jeanne—Keskoua's oldest daughter; adopted by Claude and Marguerite
(the actual daughter of Claude and "Kesk8a" and taken in and
raised by Claude and Marguerite; the author's 6th great-grandaunt)

Keskoua—thirty-nine winters in 1704 (the mother of the author's
great-grandaunt, Jeanne)

Lazare—Acadian man married to Rachelle, father of Yvonne

Little Bat—one of J-B's Spirit Questers

Little Gracie—daughter of Afia

Makena, Mak, aka "Curly"—escaped African "slave," brother of Afia
so uncle of Afia's daughter who was born in 1694 at Boston with
Gracie Waite helping (*Refuge in l'Acadie*)

Marguerite Petitpas—wife of Claude (the author's 7th great-
grandmother)

Matuwes—a resident of Mak's village who took over as Healer when
former healer was killed, a.k.a. Dit Ceci

Monsieur Hermel St-Amand—previous surgeon at the fort, now living
in Boston as Edward Gooden

Mouse—Gig's younger son, not named yet in 1704

Nation—man who captures Keskoua, see Damnation, above

Obadiah—man who captures Keskoua

Otter—Acadian man, one of the people in Flower Stalk's village

Pierre Poitou—soldier at the fort, nephew of Gabbie Grenier

Rachelle—wife of Lazare and mother of Yvonne

Second Son—troubled man from Keskoua's village, hereditary Chief, or so he claims

Singing Bear—Chief in Keskoua's village

Snowy Owl—Gig's elder son

Solange—Falcon's young girlfriend

Su´n (Cranberry)—daughter of Falcon and Keskoua

Tities (Bluejay)—son of Falcon and Keskoua

Willem KrommeZee—captain of the *Rita Petronella*

Rabbit Woman—a resident of Keskoua's village, helps Keskoua when needed as a healer

Scratchy Voice—elderly survivor at Mak's village, mother-in-law of Hawk Throat

Yvonne—daughter of Lazare and Rachelle

Zeke—man who captures Keskoua, a spy and friend of Edward Gooden

Vocabulary

apalqaqamej: chipmunk

apistanewj: marten; apistanewjig, martens (plural); apistanewjl, a marten (fourth person)

apli´kmuj: rabbit, hare; apli´gmujg, rabbits (plural); apli´gmujl, a rabbit (fourth person)

apo´qatej: woodpecker; variant spelling(s): apo´qajej (Nova Scotia), apo´qwatej; alternate forms: apo´qatejg, woodpeckers (plural); apo´qatejl, a woodpecker (fourth person)

app: repeat [please]; what did you say?

apugji´j: mouse; apigji´jg, mice (plural); apigji´jl, apigji´tl, a mouse (fourth person); variant spelling(s): apugji´j (Nova Scotia)

atu´tuej, a squirrel; atu´tuejg, squirrels (plural); aju´tuej (fourth person)

chenoo: wendigo, a mythological creature or "evil spirit"

e´e: yes

elue´wiet: crazy

gajuewj: cat

gapjagwej: robin; gapjagwejg, robins; gapjagwejl: a robin

ga´qaquj: crow

gesnugwai: I am sick (first person singular animate); gesnugwaieg, we are sick (first person dual exclusive animate); gesnugutieg, we are sick (first person plural exclusive animate)

gi´gwesu: muskrat

Giju´: Mother, Mom

giwnig: otter; giwnigaq, otters (plural); giwnigal, an otter (fourth person)

gmu´jminn, a raspberry (fourth person); gmu´jming, raspberries (plural)

gopit: beaver; gopitg, beavers (plural)

gu´gu´gwes: owl; gu´gu´gwesg, owls (plural)

guow (guaq): pine; alternate forms: guaq, pines (plural): guowl, a pine
    (fourth person)

kaksk´us, kaksk´ug: cedar(s)

kønsorganer: Danish: genitals

lentug: deer

Lnu Saqamaw: Chief

lutmaqan: gossip, rumor, hearsay

mala´sit: not doing well (health), progressing slowly

masgwi: white birch tree; masgwi´g, white birch trees (plural); masgwi´l,
    a white birch tree (fourth person)

massa, mess or mass: great

massawachusett: great mountain place

melgwisgat: nightmare; frightened (from nightmare); alternate forms:
    melgwisgai, I have a nightmare (first person singular animate);
    melgwisgaieg, we have a nightmare (first person dual exclusive
    animate); melgwisga´tieg, we have a nightmare (first person plural
    exclusive animate)

mesgei´: I am sorry

Mi´kmaw, Mi´kmaq: Eastern Nation of Aboriginal People

mi´jan: excrement

mi´watm: I am grateful; mi´watmeg: we are grateful

moqopa´q: wine

moqua´: no

mtesgm: snake; mtesgmug, snakes (plural); mtesgml, a snake (fourth
    person)

mui´n: bear

mulumgwej groundhog, woodchuck

munti: bag, sack

nalagit: energetic, swift, eager

na to´q: all right, OK

oqoti: term of endearment between spouses

paqtesmul, a wolf (fourth person); paqtesmug, wolves (plural)

sec, sac or saco: mouth

snawe´l, snawe´g: sugar tree(s), maple(s)

so´qomu´jl: a minnow (fourth person); so´qomu´jg, minnows (plural)

sqolj: frog; variant spelling(s): atagali (Nova Scotia); alternate forms:
    sqoljig, frogs (plural); sqoljl, a frog (fourth person)

su´n: cranberry

Tata´t: Father, Dad

tities: bluejay; titiesg: bluejays (plural); titiesl: a bluejay (fourth person)

tqoqwej: lynx, bobcat, wild cat; alternate forms: tqoqwejg, wild
    cats (plural); tqoqwejl, a wild cat (fourth person)

tutji´j: little daughter

wasueg: flower, blossom, bloom, [blossoming flower]

wela´lin: thank you

welaliog: thank you all